THE
SPY
BOOK

John Westin

McNeil & Richards

Published by McNeil & Richards
www.mcneilandrichards.com

| ISBN 13 | 978-0-9825602-0-4 |
| ISBN | 0982560206 |

Printed in the U.S.A.

THE SOVIET UNION did not engage in espionage. We did have many countrymen and people of foreign citizenship who wrote us occasionally, enclosing information about what was happening in various countries around the world, and we scrutinized that information very closely. But espionage? Certainly not.

— *minor K.G.B. official*
during the Gorbachev years
(now an insurance salesman)

Contents

I

Orders from Moscow

August 1990

1

August

FROM THE STREET, Billy D's automobile repair shop in Brooklyn looked like hundreds of other car repair shacks scattered across the country. Out front were two gas pumps, three beat-up cars and a sign battered by storms. But this repair shop had something the others did not have—a Soviet secret agent working in the garage, only his shoes visible under an old Ford Escort.

A humorless man wearing a cheap blue suit waited impatiently inside the garage. "My car ready?" he growled.

Nick Boorstin, a thirty-eight-year-old immigrant with unruly black hair, crawled out from under the Ford. Grease covered his tattered overalls. "You come back in hour?"

"No!" said the customer.

Nick got to his feet and wiped grease off his hands. At

five-ten he was about four inches shorter than the customer and at least sixty pounds lighter. "Well, I'm not finished. Wait here for hour?"

"No!"

Nick shrugged. "Okay. It's ready." He handed the customer the keys. The man headed into the office to pay for the repairs.

The Ford wasn't really ready, of course. Nick hadn't had time to adjust the brakes or tinker with the transmission. But what was he supposed to do? The man wanted his car immediately. If anything happened after the car left the garage, that was not Nick's concern.

Three or four minutes later, the man emerged from the office, climbed into the Ford and drove off without so much as a "thanks" or "have a nice day".

Nick kicked a wrench out of the way, getting ready for the next job, when he noticed a piece of paper stuck in his toolbox. He picked it up. It seemed to be blank, but Nick realized that on the paper probably was a hidden coded message the customer had left for him. Nick was trained to expect such things. He stuck the note in his back pocket. When lunchtime rolled around, he would return to his apartment and heat the paper to see if it contained a message from Moscow.

Sonuvabitch. So the guy was making a drop for him. The guy whose brakes were about to give out—probably in heavy traffic, maybe when he was going forty or fifty miles an hour—worked for the K.G.B., too. Well, how was Nick supposed to know? Nick assumed he was just another impatient slimeball who had wandered in off the street.

"What's next?" Nick shouted to Billy Daniels, the owner of the shop.

"Red Pontiac," Billy hollered. *"Check the brakes and the engine."*

It occurred to Nick that his job gave him a unique opportunity in decadent capitalist America. Nick could knock off the whole population of America one-by-one simply by working on their cars. Sure, it would take a while, but Nick had time. Plenty of time. Moscow only contacted him every two or three years. Supervising the K.G.B.'s moles and sleeper agents in the Northeast—and South Carolina—was a part-time gig. The agents usually didn't give him trouble. Henry in Boston kept asking for more money and every once in a while Nick had to drop off a bag of loot for him, but most of the others didn't complain.

SHORTLY AFTER NOON, Nick devoured a hamburger at Maybell's, the greasy diner down the street, then drove his beat-up Chevy two miles to the three-story brick apartment building where he lived.

As "Maude" played on the Admiral television and his cat Ivan tore up another pair of slippers in his three-room furnished apartment, Nick held the note close to a candle and a message began to reveal itself. Very good so far.

Then the note caught fire.

Panicking, Nick reached for the nearest object and tried to blot out the flames. He singed his hand, crying out in pain.

A few seconds later, he smelled something burning—and discovered the object he had used to douse the flames was his billfold, which was now burning. Nick threw the billfold into the kitchen sink, turned on the faucet—and realized the flames had damaged his driver's license, credit cards and fifty-three dollars in paper money.

He sat at the table as though in a trance while Ivan stared at him with a "you are *so* dumb" look on his face. Then Nick noticed all was not lost. He had indeed saved most of the message from being destroyed. He fetched the code book taped to the bottom of a dresser drawer in his bedroom and returned to the kitchen table, where he attempted to decipher the message, which Moscow had sent in English because Nick's Russian was rusty. On a corner of the paper was inscribed "E3", so Nick opened the code book to page E3. It was a simple code; it involved starting at the bottom right and going up one column and down the next and up the next until the message was decoded. He took another look at the message. The letters were in the middle of the page so the fire had not defaced them:

```
    N  E  H  S  S  A  V  E  M  N  A  N
 Y  R  A  E  I  A  Y  I  R  U  O  T  E
 T  O  T  L  E  P  M  V  O  S  T  A  T
 I  U  A  P  H  D  O  E  T  T  S  L  A
 R  T  D  I  M  O  N  S  W  T  R  I  V
 O  E  N  N  I  N  O  O  O  E  U  E  I
 I  T  O  G  H  T  C  V  H  L  H  P  T
 R  O  C  U  L  T  E  I  R  L  T  R  C
 P  P  E  S  L  E  T  E  E  H  F  O  A
```

In a short time, he had decoded the message in its entirety:

```
ACTIVATE NATALIE.
PROF THURSTON MUST TELL HER
HOW TO REVIVE SOVIET ECONOMY ASAP.
DON'T TELL HIM HE IS HELPING US.
ECON DATA EN ROUTE.
TOP PRIORITY.
```

So, Moscow was assigning him to oversee a project with the highest priority. Nick thought about the ramifications. If the project was a success, Nick would be praised and recognized in the highest circles of government and undoubtedly promoted and given a hefty bonus. If the project failed, Nick would be held personally responsible. That would not mean retirement and a state pension. Moscow probably would decide to eliminate Nick, and one night when he least expected it, perhaps when he was in bed with the waitress who lived in the apartment down the hall, a quiet man with a vaguely familiar face would knock down the door of his apartment, gun down Nick and Molly—what a waste, she had a nice rack on her—and then hastily retreat. Police investigating the murders would conclude that Molly's husband had slain them, for what other motive could there be?, and the poor sap would be convicted and executed, and that was all right. When Nick died, he wanted to take some people with him. Maybe that's what the shrink back in Moscow meant when she said Nick had antisocial tendencies.

Nick knew he must move on this immediately. He called Billy Daniels and told him he wouldn't be back for a day or two, that the hamburger at Maybell's diner had given him food poisoning again. Then he threw a few things into an overnight bag, and—with message in hand—climbed into his blue Chevy and headed south on Interstate 95, the first leg of his trip to Charlottesville, Virginia.

2

MORE THAN 4,600 MILES away, in a large dining room inside a Russian dacha, Soviet Union President Mikhail Gorbachev pushed his dinner plate away and mumbled, "It was good Andrei. Yes?"

"Yes," agreed Andrei unenthusiastically. It was not wise to say the shashliki needed some salt.

"Let's go to other room," Gorbachev said, as he lit up a cigar.

They settled into comfortable armchairs as a servant brought them after-dinner drinks. Gorbachev still had a supply of good vodka—one of the perks that came with his job. Rising prices had forced some Russians to resort to drinking perfume or antifreeze.

"So what you think I should do?" Gorbachev asked

Andrei, who was not only a close friend but an economic advisor. "Even after my reforms, economy collapsing. I inherited this mess, and no matter what I do, it gets worse."

Andrei shook his head. Most of the Soviet Union's economic troubles were rooted in the structure of the system adopted almost seventy years earlier. Gorbachev realized this, and was trying to make changes with his restructuring, which he called perestroika, but it was a mess. Like trying to put one small bandage on a horse that had been shot in a dozen places. Nevertheless, there was no way Andrei was going to tell the Soviet leader he believed his economic plans were doomed.

"The actions you have taken were inspired," Andrei said diplomatically.

"Maybe. Maybe not. I will tell you something. I have embarked on secret plan that might offer new ideas. I am known for willingness to try new things, and that's what I must do now. I ordered K.G.B. to find very good economist in United States who can carefully analyze our economy and come up with economic plan that will work. Must be done immediately. Time is running out. I want *you* to oversee project from this end. I call it Project Economy. Good name, yes?"

"Yes, Mr. President."

Gorbachev handed Andrei a bound report. "Details are in here. Take care of it!"

Andrei excused himself as Gorbachev nursed his vodka and gazed out a window at the nearby trees.

"Just my luck," Gorbachev muttered. "Finally got my

chance to run Soviet Union, but it's so far gone, my dream has become nightmare. Would be ironic if American economist helps me turn this mess around."

3

As Nick weaved through traffic on Highway 20 in Virginia, he tried to remember how long it had been since he had left Russia. Nearly twenty years, he decided. Long time to be away. But he was serving his Fatherland in the United States. He had prepared for his assignment at the school where the Soviet Union trained all its spies who would be sent overseas. There, he learned things that would help him assimilate into American life. He learned to eat fast food, and take antacid tablets. He learned to converse with others about television shows that rotted the brain. And he tried to learn to speak English like an American. That did not work out so good, so the K.G.B. decided Nick should not pretend to be an American; he would be an immigrant who had fled Russia for the United States. Come to think of it, he had never received his final grades from the school. Was that an oversight on the K.G.B.'s part?

Nick picked up his cell phone to call Natalie Kramer, his "mole" in Charlottesville. Such an ugly word to describe an attractive woman. She had been told that one day she would be activated. Nick would not tell her about the project over the phone—half the country might be listening in—but he needed to alert Natalie that he would meet her at their pre-arranged location. All he had to do was call her.

He could not remember her phone number.

Try, damn it, he thought. *You were trained to have excellent memory. You must remember her number!*

He never wrote down phone numbers or names of agents, always trusting his memory. And his memory had always been considered exceptional. Once he had memorized an entire page from the New York City telephone book. Later, a page of classified ads from *Newsday*. His superiors had been duly impressed. (Although one of them expressed doubts. "Why, in the name of Stalin, would any jerk memorize a page of classified ads?") But now he could not remember one lousy number. He could recall the whole page of useless New York City telephone numbers, but he could not remember Natalie's number, the one he needed so desperately.

Try again, Nick told himself. *Concentrate. Use that brilliant mind. Force yourself to remember, just as you would force others to remember if they could not think of the number.* Nick was disciplined, a hard task master. In Moscow, they still spoke of the time, during Brezhnev's rule, when Nick invited his superior in the United States to his apartment, an apartment next to rooms where a German lived, and after having sauerkraut and hot dogs for dinner, the superior said, "Maybe we should put away the kraut." Meaning the sauerkraut, of course, but Nick thought he meant the German next door. So Nick bumped off the German that night, execution-style, and it was a neat job, and despite the mixup Moscow was impressed with Nick's dedication to his job, and Nick became something of a legend in espionage circles. Now Nick had his superior's old job, controlling all the Russian "moles" in the Northeastern United States (and South Carolina). Nick took his work seriously. For fun—when Molly was busy—he would stop at pay phones and make crank calls to the C.I.A. or the National Security Agency.

His confidence bolstered by the memory of the execution of the German, Nick began to dial. Two-one-two two-nine-five eight-six ... Oh, for the love of mud, that was the number of his escape hatch, the agent he was supposed to call if he needed to get out of the country quickly. A couple more numbers and he'd be on his way to Moscow before he could explain it was all a mistake.

He tried again.

It was ringing!

"Rainbow Delicatessen. You want it, we got it."

Nick was pissed off. Perhaps he should get the address of the delicatessen and blow it to smithereens. He really didn't like the tone of the peasant's voice on the other end of the line. Well, there simply was no time for that. He hung up.

He must call his mole. Precious minutes were being wasted.

Reluctantly, despondently, he dialed another number.

"Information."

Nick sighed. He could just die. The humiliation of it all. Relying on a public, capitalistic telephone system to contact one of his spies. He could not seem to make the words come out.

"Is anyone there?" the operator asked.

"Yes, uh ... I need ... I need number ... uh ..."

"Take your time, buster. I don't go off duty for three hours."

Swine. He really ought to bump off the telephone operator, nobody would care ... but time was being wasted.

"Yes. uh ... if you could overcome your rudeness for moment, I need number in Charlottesville, Virginia, of Natalie Kramer."

Nick feared this was the beginning of the end of his long, sometimes glorious, sometimes notorious career.

And all because of a damn telephone number.

The operator gave him the number. "I knew it!" Nick cried out. "I knew it! I just couldn't think of it ... but I knew it!"

He hung up, not worrying about what the operator had thought of his outburst. He was trained not to worry about such things.

4

Natalie Kramer resided in a brick apartment house surrounded by dogwood and oak trees on a quiet residential street in Charlottesville, a city of about 50,000 people near the Blue Ridge Mountains. To her neighbors, this slender brunette seemed happy, friendly and perfectly normal—and even that had not aroused their suspicions. From conversations with her they had surmised that she liked ice cream, hamburgers, the novels and poetry of Robert Penn Warren, and a young plumber named Harry whose Pontiac often was parked in front of the apartment house.

The neighbors never had any reason to suspect she was an agent for the Soviet Union. Natalie had a hard time believing it herself, because she loved living in the United States and was very fond of Charlottesville, which was only about two miles from Monticello, Thomas Jefferson's homestead.

If Natalie had appreciated life in the United States nine years earlier, when she had been an undergraduate majoring in history at Columbia University in New York City, she never would have become a spy for the Soviet Union. But she was younger then, a radical inflamed with contempt for the injustice and inequality she saw around her, and when a boyfriend took her to a meeting of a Communist cell a few miles from the university, it had not seemed all that threatening and despicable. Nick was the coordinator at these meetings—"Moscow's stooge," some called him—and his job was similar to the snake's function in the Garden of Eden. He wanted to corrupt these idealistic young people. In Nick's case, the motive was to put them in the service of Moscow. And Nick was very good at his job. He first encouraged them to participate in rallies for just causes, rallies where the Communists were only a small minority and the youngsters felt they were doing something worthwhile. Then he gave these young Communist sympathizers tasks to do, little things that would help Moscow in a minor way but, more importantly, would involve the recruits in Communist espionage activities. Then the importance of their work escalated, and before long they were deeper into the party than they had ever imagined possible. Nick had made it clear, the last time he had seen Natalie, that one day she would be called on to provide an important service for Moscow—and if she resisted, Natalie or her mother would be "eliminated." And so Natalie had become a mole for the Soviet Union.

NATALIE WAS BRUSHING her hair when the telephone rang at a few minutes after four that August afternoon. She always felt a twinge of fear when the phone rang, even after all those years, because she never knew when Nick might call. Her life seemed to be sandwiched between telephone calls.

Rrriiiiinnnng.

She could only hope it was Harry calling. Reluctantly, she picked up the receiver.

"You want to buy cemetery plot?"

It might be Nick calling. That was the opening gambit Nick had chosen to use instead of passwords. Unfortunately, Nick, who in some ways was dull-witted and conformed to the stereotype of the plodding Russian, had chosen an opening line that a number of other people might be using. Six times in the past five years Natalie had received such calls, and by the time she found out it wasn't Nick calling, she had purchased another cemetery plot. Television commercials said one should have enough funeral plots for the entire family, but Natalie lived alone and she had six.

"I might be interested. Do you have one in my shape?"

If Nick was calling, he would know now that indeed Natalie was on the other end of the line. It was such a stupid line she was embarrassed to say it.

"Definitely. Are you in good health?"

It was Nick's way of asking if she was alone and free to talk. She wanted to hang up on him, but she was too deeply involved with Nick and the Soviets to back out gracefully.

"Good health."

"Excellent. I am glad you have a listed telephone number."

"What?"

There was a deep sigh on the other end.

"Forget it. You would not understand ... We should meet to discuss cemetery plot."

Natalie yearned to exercise the prerogative of every American and say, "No, I do not want a cemetery plot, to hell with you," but Nick would not be amused.

"I suppose so."

"Tomorrow morning. Nine o'clock. Be there."

THE NEXT MORNING, NATALIE took a shower, brushed her hair and applied lipstick. (Force of habit, Nick wasn't worth it.) After breakfast, she drove her brown Volvo through the streets of Charlottesville as she speculated about how much danger she would be in. A simple assignment, such as copying names out of newspapers, would be nice, but it was no use kidding herself. Russia didn't use its moles for such uncomplicated tasks.

5

MINUTES LATER, SHE ARRIVED at the location Nick had selected three years earlier: Monticello.

Familiar with stories describing how Thomas Jefferson had invented a device to code and decode messages, Nick thought it would be ironic and amusing if they rendezvoused at the home Jefferson had designed for himself more than two hundred years earlier.

Natalie parked the Volvo and admired the beautiful red brick neoclassical Roman home Jefferson had created. Tourists milled around the grounds. "The next tour begins in a few minutes," a white-haired lady was saying. "You may purchase your tickets now."

Nick shelled out money for his ticket and kept his distance from Natalie. She recognized him immediately. Nick would always look the same—a little plodding man who had become trapped in the spy game and would never find his way out of the maze.

SHE BOUGHT A TICKET and within a few minutes the tour of the first floor of Monticello began. The second floor was off limits because of fire regulations. Then she noticed Nick had purchased a ticket for a different tour—to see the gardens and grounds. That idiot.

When Nick realized what had happened, he shelled out more dough for a ticket to tour the house.

As the tour guide talked about various gadgets and books that had belonged to Jefferson, Nick moved closer to Natalie.

"Better be worth it," he said. "Had to buy two tickets."

As the tour guide described the architectural ornamentation, Nick guided Natalie into a side room.

"Your time has come! You have opportunity to perform great service for the Fatherland!"

"My Fatherland is the United States," she pointed out.

"Okay. Great service for *my* Fatherland—Soviet Union."

He noticed a surveillance camera focused on them. "Maybe this was not good idea. Everywhere, there are cameras. What's the matter? Don't people trust me?"

"Nick, you're a Russian agent. Why should people trust you?"

"Yes, but they don't know that."

"What do you want, Nick?"

"Back home they are having troubles with economy."

"That's putting it mildly. I read things are so bad Gorby turned his dacha into a bed and breakfast."

"*Gorby? You call our great leader, Comrade Gorbachev, Gorby?*"

"There are a few other things I could call him."

"I suggest you show respect! Remember what we can do to you and your mother if you do not cooperate. Besides, he has *not* turned it into bed and breakfast. He sometimes has overnight guests, but I am sure they do not pay!"

"What do you want, Nick?"

"Moscow has important assignment for you. *Very* important. Why they want *you* to do it, I do not know."

"Get to the point, Nick."

"They want you to convince professor at university here—name is Thurston— to analyze why Soviet economy is in trouble and tell them how to change things."

"They might try capitalism."

"Very funny. Keep your sense of humor. You'll need it in Soviet prison. Things they do to women like you, they are not pretty."

"How am I supposed to get Thurston's help?"

"That is up to you. Just do it. By the way ..." He handed her a sack he was carrying. "In here is a wheel cipher."

"A real cipher?"

"No! A *wheel cipher!* Since Thomas Jefferson invented it, thought we would use it to exchange messages. I made two of these. One for you, one for me. Took two, three months."

She peered into the sack. "This thing looks complicated!"

"Instruction book is in sack. One more thing. I passed Last Chance Motor Lodge on way into the city. We'll use

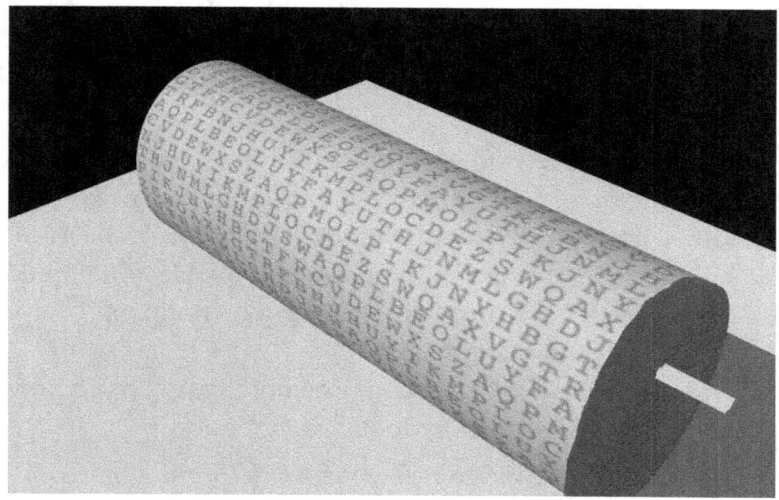

bench in front as our dead drop when we need to communicate."

"You like this cloak and dagger stuff, don't you, Nick?"

"This is very serious business. One mistake, we wind up in prison! ... Okay, let's get back to tour. Is very interesting."

NICK DISAPPEARED BEFORE the tour ended. Natalie made her way to the parking area, climbed into her Volvo and drove back into the city, turning onto a street winding past large old houses with massive lawns. The assignment from Moscow was very confusing. How was she supposed to secure the professor's help without his knowledge? And yet, it must be that way, for she did not want to put the professor's life in jeopardy. Or hers.

She drove slowly back to her house. It had not been a good week. First, the kitchen sink had plugged up, and that annoyed her. Then Moscow activated her, and somehow the sink did not seem very important.

Later that day, she signed up for two of Professor Eugene Thurston's economics classes.

II

New on Campus

September 1990

6

THE FOLLOWING TUESDAY, Professor Eugene Thurston strolled past dogwood trees and vintage red brick buildings on his way to Monroe Hall, which housed the Economics Department at the University of Virginia. With each step, Thurston imagined he was being drawn further into America's past, back to the early years, when the country was young and the university a mere infant. Thomas Jefferson had founded the institution and designed the original buildings—the Rotunda and the pavilions on either side of the Rotunda. His presence was still felt on campus. Thurston almost expected to see Jefferson coming down the walkway, saying, "Morning, Thurston. Let's meet for tea later. I have some new ideas for the university in mind, and I want to discuss them with you."

"Sure thing, Tom. I've got a few ideas of my own."

IT WAS A BREEZY, SUNNY and warm day, not unusual for Charlottesville in the autumn, and Thurston was full of energy. He felt twenty-seven instead of forty-two, and the pessimism he had experienced in recent months about where the American economy and government were heading was temporarily forgotten.

Grasping his lecture notes—God forbid that such knowledge should be lost, future generations might be doomed—Thurston hurried on, occasionally nodding to other professors, instructors, or students, sometimes stopping to converse for a few moments. He was well known on campus, though his star had dimmed in recent years. During the Carter presidency, Thurston frequently traveled to Washington to consult on economic policy. Now, in exile during the ascendancy of Reaganomics and conservative economists, Thurston had been relegated to being a critic of the Establishment as some of his colleagues advised government officials on economic policy. So be it. May God dump snow on them and may they feel a hundred and twenty years old. (Buried deep inside every economist was a little bit of the witch doctor.)

Thurston nodded to a shapely brunette about to enter the lecture hall and strode professorially to the front, hoping to impress the students with his charm, intelligence, dignity and Southwick suit. No surveys had been taken to indicate whether students who habitually wore jeans and sweatshirts were impressed by professors wearing custom-made suits, but it was worth a try.

NATALIE KRAMER CLAIMED a seat on the north side of the room, about fifteen feet away from Thurston. She was older than most of the students, but that did not stop young men seated nearby from making advances. She tried to seem disinterested and unattainable, but that did not quiet their hormones.

As the professor approached the lectern, Natalie noted he was more handsome than the photo of him in the Economics Department brochure suggested. The profile next to the photo noted that Thurston had been born in Chicago, graduated from the University of Chicago, received a master's degree at Minnesota and taught at Princeton before joining the University of Virginia economics faculty. Natalie was duly impressed when she read Thurston had worked with President Carter's team of economic advisers. The profile mentioned Thurston liked Chinese food, suspense movies and economic theory. One last piece of information had been provided by an undergrad who signed up for courses at the same time Natalie did: Thurston was divorced. He and his wife, Cynthia, had split after fourteen years of marriage.

"LET'S GET STARTED. I AM Professor Thurston and this is Economics 1225, Old Theories, New Realities. If you are in the wrong place, now is the time to leave."

One young man with long stringy hair headed for the exit.

"I hope it wasn't something I said."

The class laughed.

"I have seen professors spend half of the first class discussing housekeeping matters, so let's get that out of the way quickly: your grade depends on two quizzes, the final exam and class discussion. My office hours are three to four on Tuesday mornings. If I am not there—which I won't be—assume I left for a cup of coffee and that I'll be right back. The required text is a magnificent work you may have heard of: *Adam Smith Doesn't Live Here Anymore* by Eugene J. Thurston." He held up a copy of the book. "It is available at the University Bookstore, or if you don't feel like contributing to my retirement fund, reasonably priced used copies can be found floating around bookstores. Any questions? I didn't think so.

"In this class, we will investigate whether traditional economic theories adequately explain today's economic conditions. Where do time-tested theories fall short in describing what is actually happening in the world today? Our goal is to question accepted dogma and see things more clearly, and to consider whether economists have even the faintest idea what is going on in the world today. Present company excepted, of course."

It received the laugh he had anticipated. It was his equivalent of a standup comedian warming up his audience. A few professors could command the attention of students simply through the sheer weight of their learning and achievements, but Thurston had not reached that stage. Perhaps another tour of duty in Washington would do it.

"Of course, my prejudices, forged in the steel furnaces of real life, affect my outlook on these things, as do yours.

By playing the devil's advocate instead of embracing prevailing economic doctrine, I hope to stimulate thought and provoke interesting discussions. I will offer ideas about the shortcomings of traditional economic theories, and it is your responsibility to challenge me by defending those theories or offering insights of your own. Then, of course, my superior knowledge will destroy your challenges and we shall proceed on to the next subject of study."

They laughed again, only Thurston wasn't joking. Or at least, he didn't think he was. He noticed the attractive woman he had passed on the way into the classroom was attentive and had a pleasant smile. Just having her in class would make it more interesting for him. Professors weren't supposed to play favorites, but Thurston and most of his colleagues looked forward to seeing shapely members of the opposite sex in class each week. They tried not to let their bias show in class, but it was there, just the same.

"As we proceed through the course, the elephant in the room will be the economic theories that have been dominant in Washington over the last nine years or so—sometimes called Reaganomics, supply side economics, or voodoo economics. Although it's unfortunate for the country that economists who value defense spending more than the well-being of the people are in the saddle in Washington, it is not a bad thing for this class, for they provide a large and inviting target as we investigate where economic theories succeed and where they fail. There is a great deal of room to argue with Ronald Reagan's budgetary decisions. He doubled the military budget, giving the Pentagon everything it wanted and more, while talking about the terrible economic shape the country was in, and using that as an excuse to cut billions of dollars from social programs that helped people. He cut taxes to stimulate the economy, he said; his tax cuts helped the rich immensely but did little for the economy or the lower economic classes. The budget deficit increased sharply, and some believe Reagan intentionally increased the debt so he could argue that there was no money to fund social programs.

"But let's not get into all that today. In the weeks to come, we also will examine how political ideologies affect economic theories. My contention is that dogmatic political ideas prevent people from seeing what is really going on in the world, whether the dogmatism comes from communists, socialists, Reagan conservatives, or any other captives of ideology."

Thurston glanced at the class enrollment list and decided, by a process of elimination, that the fetching older student must be Natalie Kramer. Then he realized the class was waiting on him to continue.

He rambled on for another twenty minutes, then glanced at the clock and announced, "Well, that's enough for today. Read the first three chapters in my book for next week."

Several students crowded around Thurston as he gathered his notes. Some merely wanted to tell him they were switching into or out of his class—he really didn't give a damn, but perhaps he should—and others wanted to ask his opinions about books, theories, or other classes they could take instead of his. A few were shameless sycophants who hoped to impress him by asking intelligent-sounding questions, or offering their own seemingly insightful observations about the class. He felt sorry for them. They did not realize it took more than that to impress a veteran of academic wars. In recent years, the only student whose behavior had attracted his attention was a young woman who, under the influence of having just seen the classic Elliott Gould film *Getting Straight*, tore off her blouse and screamed, "I'm tired of this academic bullshit. Nobody here knows anything about anything!" He took her to lunch.

Thurston was pleased to notice the woman he had christened Natalie Kramer was waiting to talk to him. Quickly, he took care of the others, all except one particularly pesky, studious young man.

"I want to do some extra reading for this class. What do you recommend?"

Thurston's eyes were on Miss Kramer as he talked to the young man. "I'll hand out a bibliography at the next class session."

"I'd like to get started on the reading *now*," the student insisted, as though his entire future depended on it.

"Oh, hell, kid, I don't know. Start with my book. I'll suggest more reading next week."

The young man seemed shocked that a professor would treat him so brusquely. He mumbled "all right" and made his way to the door. Only Thurston and Natalie remained in the classroom.

"And what can I do for you?" Thurston asked,

"Well, I'm not going to ask for suggestions on extra reading."

Thurston smiled. "I'm usually not that rude. At least not until the third or fourth week of the semester."

"My name is Natalie Kramer, and—"

"How nice."

"Uh, yes. I was wondering, Professor Thurston ... you see, I want to write a book on the massive economic problems facing the Soviet Union—"

"Interesting."

"—but I'm going to need a lot of help. I don't even know how to get started. Since you don't seem to encourage visitors during office hours, I was wondering if we could have dinner one evening to talk about it. I know it's terribly presumptuous."

Thurston smiled. He had not expected her to propose dinner. Female students were usually shy about such things, even though Natalie was older than most co-eds.

"That might be very nice."

"Perhaps you could come to my apartment tomorrow night and we could talk about it."

Miracles will never cease, Thurston thought.

"Yes, I could do that."

Natalie smiled. "Six o'clock?" she asked, as she wrote the address on a piece of paper for him.

"Fine," Thurston said.

He watched as she sashayed to the exit, hips swaying. What would it take, he wondered, to arouse Miss Kramer's passions to the point where *she* would tear off her blouse?

Yes, the new semester might be one of the most interesting in years.

7

THE NEXT AFTERNOON, AS Thurston crossed campus on his way to a meeting of Economics Department faculty, his mind explored possible relationships with Natalie Kramer. How did it happen that on the first day of class she had approached him with the intriguing proposition that he visit her apartment? What was the catch? Was she desperate for a good grade? Was she trying to set him up, having someone take pictures of them in a compromising position? Or, was Natalie some kind of weirdo who stalked professors and stashed their dead bodies in her apartment?

On the other hand, was it really surprising that she should be interested in him? After all, Thurston was a rather well-known professor. Why wouldn't a woman of Natalie's age and sophistication throw herself at him? Didn't he possess charm, intelligence, maturity and a certain sexuality? Considered from that perspective, Natalie's loss of control during the first class session was perfectly understandable.

Who was he kidding? The whole thing was surprising, all right. It had surprised the hell out of *him*. This kind of thing had never before happened to him on the first day of class. *Thurston,* he muttered, *you're not getting older, you're getting better.*

"Talking to yourself again, Gene?"

Glen McCracken, a colleague in the Economics Department, interrupted Thurston's reverie. McCracken, a lean man in his mid-forties, was the department's expert in the areas of game theory, probability and developing countries.

"Was I? Damn. Do you think anyone else noticed?"

"Probably. I heard your ramblings when I was six feet away."

Thurston shook his head. "That's bad. This would be the first indication to students and colleagues that I might be fallible. It could ruin my image."

McCracken smiled as they continued on toward Monroe Hall. "I hate to rain on your parade, Gene, but your image isn't spotless. You're thinking of Christ's image."

"That's the trouble with being someone in my position. I've got to endure taunts and petty barbs from someone in *your* position."

"Ironic, isn't it?"

"What, McCracken?"

"You teach a class about how old economic theories are out of touch with reality—and yet, you are obviously out of touch with reality. Ironic, indeed. ... It's fortunate for you that I know you aren't as much of a pompous ass as you pretend to be. Now there ..." McCracken nodded toward one of their colleagues, Herbert Winston, who was also converging on Monroe Hall, "is a real pompous ass."

As Winston drew near, McCracken said, "Hello, Herbert."

"Well, if it isn't the apostle of the socialist state"—Winston nodded at Thurston—"and the synthesizer of outdated economic theories!"—he nodded at McCracken.

Thurston sighed. "That's amusing, coming from the department's advocate for greed, the military state and shoddy economic theories."

"Care to join us for a drink after the meeting?" suggested McCracken.

"No time," Winston said. "Got to catch a commuter flight to Washington. That's where things are happening, you know!"

"Really," said Thurston. "I thought with Republicans in power, economic policy was hammered out in oil company boardrooms and right-wing think tanks."

"Nice seeing you, too, Thurston," Winston mumbled, as Winston entered the conference room ahead of them.

"A pompous ass indeed," Thurston said. "Before he started commuting to Washington he was just an ass."

Thurston and McCracken took seats near the door. Raymond Yardley, the department chairman, was already seated at the table, as were eleven of their colleagues in the department.

Thurston nodded toward the black-haired, middle-aged

woman seated two seats down from the chairman. "Benson showed up. First department meeting she's been to in years. Thought she retired."

"No. She had a distinguished teaching position at Stanford last year."

"Really? They must be handing out those things in cereal boxes."

Yardley called the meeting to order. "Before we get to the important matter at hand, I have two announcements. First, the custodial staff would like to ask that if you throw liquor into the waste receptacles, please make sure it is still in the bottle. Makes a mess if it is not, apparently."

"That mean you, Thurston," growled Winston.

"That means *all of you*," noted Dean Yardley. "Also, it seems someone has been stealing the toilet paper from the restrooms and taking it home."

Thurston smiled. "I believe that would be Professor Benson."

Benson, who apparently had been thinking about something else, suddenly paid more attention to what was being said. "What? Why, I never .... I did no such thing!"

"Relax, Anna," Yardley said. "Thurston is trying to yank your chain. ... In a way, such conflict in our department is related to the first order of business. We are embarking on a new semester, and that gives us a chance to turn over a new leaf, and make a clean break with the past. ..."

"Congratulations, Yardley," said Thurston. "You managed to use two clichés in one sentence. You're moving up in the world!"

"Be that as it may, Thurston. I was trying to make a point. Last year, the conflicts within the department were disruptive, and detrimental to our department in many ways, including the tarnishing of our image. Let's do better this year! The students and the university deserve more from us!

"Now, the main order of business is an announcement. I wanted to tell you about it before you read it in the newspapers. I am retiring as department chairman at the end of this academic year."

Murmurs of shock were heard around the room.

"Frankly I am weary of the academic wars. I have been chairman for thirteen years. It is time for someone else to take over. I fervently hope the new chairman will lead our department to even greater achievements while eliminating petty conflicts. Dean Pensky will consider candidates to succeed me and will select my successor."

Freida Pensky was dean of the College and Graduate School of Arts and Sciences

"I have no idea if she will go outside the department, but I am well aware we have qualified candidates within the department. I am also aware there are others within the department who would like to be chairman so they could outshine their colleagues, and use it as a steppingstone to God knows what."

"Sound familiar, Thurston?" asked Benson.

"In any case," Yardley continued, "the decision as to who will be the new chairman is out of my hands, so it will do you no good to pester me about the matter or threaten to blackmail me. Those of you who are interested in the position may now begin your campaigns to succeed me. Keep it civil. And God help us all."

Herbert Winston was the first to rush up to shake Yard-ley's hand and wish him well as the meeting came to an end. "You have been an inspiration to us all!"

"The sucking up has begun," McCracken told Thur-ston.

8

WHEN THE DEPARTMENT meeting broke up, Thurston and McCracken strolled across campus in the direction of West Main Street and the Hungry Peasant, a pub they occasionally frequented.

"That's a shock," McCracken said. "Had no idea Yardley is retiring."

"This is serious," Thurston told him. "The department could fall into the hands of extremists. Someone like Winston."

"That pompous ass ..."

"We already agreed on that."

"You interrupted me. I was making a statement."

"Sorry."

"That pompous ass would make things miserable for the rest of us—anyone to the left of Attila the Hun. He'd turn the department into a propaganda arm for supply siders. Moderation isn't in his vocabulary."

"That's why he's got to be stopped," Thurston said. "I certainly can't do it. I do not suffer fools gladly, and despite my best efforts, it sometimes shows. Besides, most of the department thinks I fly to Cuba every weekend to play checkers with Castro. ... *You* would make a good chairman, Glen. You're middle of the road. Get along with most people. A peacemaker. Besides, having you as chairman would give me more influence in the department."

"No, it wouldn't. I'd have to pretend I don't know you, like Yardley does. A chairman must be careful about whom he associates with. Above reproach, like Caesar's wife."

"Give me a break. Yardley has a gambling habit, and rumor has it he's into drugs."

"Yes, but he doesn't associate with you. Thus, his reputation is intact. Besides, there are many reasons I don't want the job. For one thing, it sounds like work. For another, people around here seem to frown on putting someone in charge who can't get his personal finances in order."

"But Winston is an egotistical airhead. You've got to try to stop him!"

"What about Durell? He's wanted the job for years."

"That's the trouble. Long on ambition, short on ability."

"There's always Billings."

"Boring. Half his students fall asleep before he gets five minutes into a lecture."

"What about Benson?"

"Too aggressive. Besides, do you really want a department chairwoman whose hobby is stealing toilet paper?"

"You shouldn't spread rumors like that, Gene. It might come back to haunt you."

"Well, think it over, Glen. Take your time. Only the future of the department, the university and the country are at stake."

"Well, as long as you aren't putting pressure on me. ..."

BEFORE STRONG WINDS BLEW the roof off and took out half the dining area, the Hungry Peasant had the quaint look of an English pub. The owners rebuilt it, but it never seemed the same to its old clientele, people like Thurston and McCracken.

The two professors seated themselves in the beech wood chairs. Thurston ordered a beer, McCracken a glass of milk.

When the waitress brought the milk, McCracken stared at it with disdain. "Damn ulcer. I remember when I could devour three or four martinis without blinking an eye."

"Which made your stomach what it is today."

McCracken shrugged. "I suppose so. ... Each time a new semester rolls around I feel older, wiser and unhappier. I feel further removed, in age and spirit, from those voluptuous coeds who make the campus their breeding ground. It's a sad thing, Gene."

Thurston smiled slyly. "Speak for yourself. You should have seen what happened in my class yesterday. A very attractive woman, a little older than the other students, threw herself at me ... literally *threw herself at me!*"

Thurston paused to let that sink in.

"Did the impact kill anyone?" asked McCracken.

"You don't believe me, but it's true, so don't tell me how old we're getting, Glen. I feel younger than ever."

"Sometimes you act it, too."

"How is Emily?" Thurston asked. Emily was McCracken's wife of fifteen years.

"She's got me on a tight budget again. She takes care of the family finances, and we're always broke. Damn embarrassing for an economics professor."

"Why? The country is wallowing in debt and you don't lose sleep over that."

"I'm talking microeconomics. I have no control over the national debt. I'll let Winston lose sleep over that."

McCracken asked Thurston what he had heard from his old friends in Washington.

"What do I hear?" Thurston repeated, eying his beer. "I'll tell you what I hear. Greed and selfishness are in the saddle. Liberals have been proclaimed an endangered species. When one dies, they don't bury him—they stuff him and put him on display in the Senate chambers. That's what I hear from Washington."

McCracken nodded. "That's what I hear, too. ... And Winston is the one doing the stuffing."

McCracken ordered another round of beer and milk.

The professors nursed their drinks. After a few minutes, McCracken said, "You say this woman ... you say she threw herself at you?"

Thurston nodded.

"What's her angle?"

"What do you mean, 'what's her angle?' She finds me irresistible."

"Compared to what?"

"Don't be a boor. She sees the real me."

McCracken took a long sip of milk. "No, she's got to have an angle. As an economist you know everyone has an angle. Self-interest rules the world."

"Natalie is different. I don't think she has an angle. She is completely guileless."

"And you are completely naive. Obviously, you were made for each other."

9

NICK WAS BACK IN Brooklyn, disabling cars belonging to capitalists in the guise of repairing them. Only about 190 million more to go and he would have the whole country incapacitated.

During his lunch break he braved thirty-mile-an-hour winds and sheets of rain to call Charlottesville from the pay phone down the street from the repair shop. He was proud of himself. He remembered Natalie's telephone number without any trouble this time. The telephone was ringing ...

"Hello?"

It was then Nick realized he did not remember the exact words of his opening gambit. Oh, God.

"Is anyone there?" Natalie asked.

Nick had to say something. Natalie would hang up if he didn't say something.

"Uh ... I would like to sell you a cemetery plot."

"NO, I DO NOT WANT a cemetery plot, to hell with you!" Natalie felt good, just being able to say it for once, just knowing it was not Nick calling, for Nick would have used the right wording. Unless ... unless he had forgotten it. Fear set in; perhaps it was Nick that she just told off.

"To hell with me?" the caller said. "You say to hell with me? Who are *you* to tell me to go to hell?"

Natalie gulped and said quietly, "Is that you, Nick?"

Nick waited a moment. "Yeah," he said finally, "it's me."

"Why didn't you use the right words?"

"Because I could not remember the damn right words."

"Oh."

There was an uneasy silence as rain falling out of the heavens drenched Nick.

"Do you have a reason for calling, Nick, or did you just want to hear my voice?"

"Don't be smart aleck. Of course I had reason for calling. I got another message."

"From Moscow?"

"Shut up. Your phone could be tapped ..." What the hell. "Yes, from Moscow. They're pushing us on this project. You'd think fate of country depended on it. They say Soviet Union economic problems getting worse. More people drinking vodka to forget about economic problems. Now price of vodka has gone up ... We must act quickly. Did you receive package I sent?"

"Package? Oh, Nick. You remembered my birthday. How sweet!"

Nick ground his teeth together. He was getting pounded by what felt like a damn hurricane and she was making jokes. "I did *not* remember your birthday. You know package I'm talking about ... facts on economy."

"Oh, I remember. No, I haven't."

At that moment, Natalie's doorbell rang. "Wait a minute," she told Nick. She opened the door and a scruffy looking delivery man handed her a package. "Thank you," Natalie said. She closed the door and returned to the telephone.

"I just received the package."

"Did you tip delivery man?"

"Tip him? No, I forgot."

"That was Boris. One of my people. I don't pay him much. He likes to be tipped. You should have given him tip."

"I'm sorry, Nick. I just didn't think of it."

"Don't know how long I can keep Boris if my agents don't tip him ... Look, you and professor must work on data. Let me know how it's going."

"All right. Goodbye, Nick."

"Happy birthday," Nick grumbled.

"Oh, that's sweet. But it's not my birthday."

Nick slammed down the telephone. Whatever happened to secrecy? Whatever happened to spies who knew what they were doing?

Whatever happened to tipping?

10

DETERMINED NOT TO appear overeager, Thurston parked his Mercury in front of Natalie's apartment house at three minutes after six. He carefully avoided stepping on a young man sprawled across the sidewalk—evidently an undergrad who had welcomed the new semester by getting drunk—and made his way to the entrance, pausing only briefly to determine if the undergrad was one of his students. The face was not familiar.

Once inside the apartment house, Thurston climbed a flight of stairs and located apartment 203.

He punched the doorbell. Moments later, Natalie stood before him in a red silk blouse with plunging neckline and tight-fitting white slacks. Her hair flowed down her neck.

"Professor Thurston. Come in."

"Call me Gene. ... Nice place you have here."

"Thanks." She motioned toward the couch. "Make yourself comfortable. Dinner will be ready shortly."

She retreated to the kitchen. "Did you think it was terribly forward of me to ask you to come here, Gene?"

"Not at all. ... Do you have a deep interest in economics?"

"Yes. I took economics classes at Columbia. That was a few years ago. Six years later, I was working in an office and going nowhere, so I knew it was time to do more with my life. I decided to work towards a masters degree. I considered several universities, but was particularly attracted to Charlottesville. And, of course, I wanted to study *under you.*"

Thurston choked. "How nice," he managed to say.

She hurried in with a glass of water. "Do you like Chinese food?" she asked.

"Love it."

"Good. Cantonese or Szechwan?"

"I would kill for Cantonese. I would die for Szechwan."

Natalie smiled. "I'm not sure what that means."

"I like them both. What are we having?"

"Spaghetti."

"What?" The apartment had the strong aroma of Chinese food.

As she hurried back to the kitchen she said, "just kidding, Gene. We're having Szechwan."

"Bless you."

From the kitchen her voice drifted in. "You are the most famous man who has ever been inside this house."

"Oh? Hasn't Richard Nixon been around to clean the windows lately?"

"What did you say?"

"Nothing. A small joke."

She returned and placed bowls of dan dan noodles and Kung Pao chicken on the dining room table. "He was here," she said. "When he left, the windows were perfectly clear. Tell me, how was it in Washington during the Carter years?"

Thurston approached the table. "Like most professors, I found being near the heart of power addictive. ... Well, to be honest, I wasn't very near the heart of power. I was off in one of the little arteries, scribbling numbers on a pad of paper and trying to look like I knew what I was doing."

"Would you like a mai tai?"

"That would be wonderful."

THE FOOD WAS NEARLY as good as the Szechwan cuisine Thurston had indulged in when he visited Los Angeles. As Natalie cleared away the dishes, he relaxed contentedly on the couch.

The phone rang and Natalie picked it up. "Hello? ... No, Harry. This isn't a good time. You must trust me."

"We've got to talk," said the voice on the phone. "I'll be right over."

"No, Harry! Not now. Not tonight!"

But he had hung up.

"Is there a problem?" asked Thurston.

"No. That was the plumber." Natalie quickly changed the subject as she settled in next to Thurston on the couch. "The book I mentioned ..."

"Yes?"

"On the Soviet economy ... It is such a massive subject, I don't know where to get started. But I have access to a great deal of detailed research."

Natalie reached for the package Nick had sent and handed a pile of papers to Thurston. He skimmed through them.

"A lot of detail indeed. Where did you get these?"

"From an acquaintance who has friends inside the Soviet Union."

"It would take a lot of time simply to organize the information ... separating what's relevant and what isn't."

Natalie moved closer. "I knew you would understand."

He looked into her eyes and felt lost. "I feel as though we've known each other a long time."

"You're sweet, Thursty ... I don't have enough expertise to write this book without help, but it could be a very important work. Don't you agree?"

Thurston took one of her hands in his. "Your skin is soft, like a baby's skin."

"Slow down, Thursty. We've only just met and you're already in the deep end of the pool. ... Like I was saying ... this book is very important to me. And the thought of spending so many evenings alone in my apartment working on it discourages me. What can I do?"

"Lonely evenings, huh?"

"That's right."

"Here ... in your apartment."

"Yes."

"Hmm. I may have a solution to your problem, my dear. You might be able to convince me to spend those lonely evenings with you. It could be a very rewarding experience for both of us. I've been looking for a project because ... well, you know, the old publish or perish thing. Faculty must produce original works or risk being left behind as others plunge ahead. We might be able to ... uh ... collaborate on this. You and me."

She moved closer, her lips nearly touching his. "How can I convince you, Thursty?"

"Well, you might try asking me."

"Oh, Thursty! Would you help me?"

He kissed her. "I would love to."

She kissed him. "You're wonderful! You saved my life!"

Thurston pulled her closer. "Nothing I wouldn't do for any beautiful woman who knows how to cook Chinese food." They kissed again. "I want you, Natalie," he whispered, breathing heavily.

"Thursty, I'm not sure we should ..."

"Natalie ..."

"But Thursty, you're just overheated."

"Damn near a raging fire."

He held her close, and kissed her passionately. Her body was lithe and smooth, her breasts even larger than he had imagined. He tried to be gentle with her, but that didn't seem to satisfy her entirely. Why was she saying, "More, Harry"? Wasn't Harry the plumber? Thurston became rougher, and she responded.

EVERYTHING IS GOING according to plan, Natalie thought. Project Economy could move ahead.

Suddenly feelings of guilt and sadness overwhelmed her. What was happening to her life? Why had she agreed to involve Thurston?

I'm sorry, Thursty, she thought. *It can't be helped. Enjoy yourself and do not ask too many questions, for I do not want them to kill you.*

A POUNDING ON THE door interrupted them.

"Natalie! Open up! I know you're in there!"

"Who's that?" asked Thurston.

"Harry."

"The plumber? Sounds angry. Didn't you pay your bill?"

The pounding got louder, rattling the living room.

"I'd better talk to him before he breaks down the door," Natalie said.

"Good idea."

She slipped outside the apartment and faced Harry in the hall.

"What do you think you're doing?" Natalie demanded.

"You're seeing someone else!"

"Calm down, Harry. I've got to write a lengthy paper for one of my classes and a classmate and I are collaborating on it. That's all there is to it, but that's why I won't be able to see you much. Besides, I think it's time we ended it. We don't have much in common."

"But Natalie!"

"It's for the best, Harry."

He clenched his teeth. "If you're lying to me, and fooling around with someone else, I'll string him up on one of the oak trees out front!"

"Harry, get a grip. It's over. Go away!"

"Not until I find out why you're dumping me!"

"I told you the truth, Harry. Deal with it!"

Harry stomped away and Natalie returned to the sofa.

"Did you hear?" Natalie asked.

"Would have been impossible not to. Especially that part about stringing me up on one of the oak trees."

"Harry has some unresolved problems."

"If I were you, I'd find a new plumber."

"I already have," she said, as she kissed her professor.

As Thurston let his passion get the better of him again, an idea occurred to Natalie. If Harry thought Nick was the one screwing around with Natalie, perhaps Harry would knock off Nick. Harry would be arrested for murder, and she would be rid of both of them. Hmm. Definitely an interesting idea. She would give it a little more thought.

III

University Days

October-December 1990

11

October

By early October, Natalie and Professor Thurston had organized the research notes from Moscow, outlined their book and started writing the first chapter. Thurston enjoyed the venture and was satisfied with the progress they were making, but Natalie was not, for some reason he did not understand. She always wanted to work harder and faster on the manuscript.

"What's the rush?" Thurston asked one evening, after indulging in a roast Natalie had cooked. "Everything is coming along well."

"A friend of mine at Rutgers says a professor there is writing a book about the Russian economy. If his book is published first, no one will pay any attention to ours."

That made sense, so Thurston plugged away on the book, not realizing it was actually a Soviet agent who was putting the pressure on Natalie.

IN MID-OCTOBER, THURSTON and McCracken and about fifty thousand other people gathered in Scott Stadium on a sunny and cool Saturday afternoon to see the University of Virginia football team battle the University of Maryland Terrapins. The Maryland backs tore through the Virginia defensive line like hungry gorillas on a rampage and the Cavaliers lost, 31 to 12. Afterwards, surrounded by disappointed fans looking for destinations where they could get drunk, Thurston and McCracken made their way to the Hungry Peasant.

As they waited for their roast beef sandwiches, beer and milk, McCracken eyed the crowd in the pub warily. "Do you think they hold me responsible?"

"For what?"

"For losing the game. I flunked our fullback last year, and he left school. He's playing for Nebraska now."

"I'm sure no one blames you," Thurston assured his colleague.

A stocky undergrad in a Virginia sweater apparently heard their conversation. "*Would have won if Crowley was still our fullback!*" the undergrad declared.

"Or maybe not," said Thurston. "But one good player wouldn't have saved our team today. It would have taken a half dozen."

"*What good would it do?*" the undergrad piped up. "*McCracken would have flunked all of them!*"

"The kid certainly holds a grudge," Thurston noted.

"It wasn't my fault Crowley was dumb," McCracken said. "He should have taken something easy, like basket weaving, or one of your classes."

"No need to get nasty, McCracken."

"Sorry. ... So how are the late-night sessions with Miss what's her name going?"

"Very well. I'm feeling much more fulfilled now."

"I'm so glad. You made my life more miserable, but you're feeling fulfilled. How nice."

"What are you talking about?"

"As you know, there are two roads to success in our department. One is being a power player, commuting to Washington, consulting with the administration in power. Washington doesn't want me, since I disagree with everything going on there, so that's out. The other is the publish or perish thing ... I planned to publish a little paper in a few months on 'Price Structures in the Steel Industry', but thanks to people like you who are writing books, my paper will look like pretty small potatoes by comparison."

"I should think so."

"And so I can either fade into the sunset or write a book of my own. All is not lost, however. My seven-year-old son suggests I write a book about penguins."

"So, you're complaining because you've got to get off your ass and do some work?"

"No! ... Not exactly ... I suppose so. Do you know of any women like Natalie who might want to spend their evenings with me?"

"Afraid not, Glen. You're on your own. Besides, Emily might have a problem with that."

"Yes. Every little thing that brings me enjoyment, she has a problem with."

"Adultery isn't a little thing."

"I suppose you're right. ... I've got an idea! Maybe your book can be divided into two books. I could take over one, you the other."

"Sorry, Glen."

"By the way, have you found a publisher yet?"

"It's a little early in the game for that."

"Not at all. Next thing you'll know, you'll have a manuscript on your hands and no one to publish it. You could waste months or years looking for a publishing house."

LATER THAT EVENING, IN the comfort of the living room in his home, Thurston took McCracken's advice and wrote letters to four publishing houses, describing the manuscript on the Russian economy—which he titled *End of the Road: the Collapse of the Soviet Economy*—and listing his academic credentials and Natalie's. He didn't bother contacting Lansmoore Publishing, the house that had issued his first book. It lost money and his editor had been rather petty about it, telling him not to call her again. Ever.

Thurston decided not to tell Natalie he was casting a net in the murky waters of commerce in hopes of bagging a publishing house. She had no experience in finding publishers for economics books and had no idea how difficult it could be. Besides, if he succeeded in landing a publisher, it would be a pleasant surprise for her.

12

THURSTON HATED HALLOWEEN parties, but he had promised Glen McCracken he would show up at the annual Halloween bash hosted by McCracken and his wife. Thurston insisted Natalie accompany him. He told her he planned to go as Sherlock Holmes. She could pick out any costume she wished.

As they dressed for the party on Halloween night, Thurston slipped on a cape and retrieved the curved pipe and deerstalker hat he had purchased. "Do I look like Sherlock Holmes?"

"You look like Gene Thurston with a pipe."

"Close enough."

Natalie slipped into a skimpy dress that revealed most of her legs and suggested clearly her ample bosom.

"Very alluring," Thurston said. "Who are you supposed to be?"

"Irene Adler. The love of Sherlock Holmes' life."

"Holmes admired Irene for her intellect. You look a little slutty."

She threw her arms around him. "Oh, Gene, you say the most romantic things."

In Thurston's maroon Mercury, Natalie kissed Thurston again. She didn't notice that Nick and Boris were watching her from the front seat of Boris' van, which was parked seventy feet away. Moscow had sent another bundle of top secret economic data to Nick and he had decided to deliver it to Natalie himself.

"Terrific," Nick mumbled. "Fooling around while Soviet Union sinks. She should be ashamed. Must tell Moscow."

"Good," Boris said. "And ask Moscow why Boris hasn't been paid since July."

"They got no money to pay us. Why you think I work in repair shop?"

"Thought you liked screwing up cars."

"Well, that's the other reason."

The van followed as Thurston drove Natalie to the McCrackens' split level ranch home on the outskirts of the city. Thurston parked down the street from the house. Several other people were on their way to the party ... Spider-man, a giant pumpkin, two skeletons, a ghost and Chucky.

Nick wanted to talk to Natalie but it was obvious he

needed a costume if he was going to get close to her. "Drive me to discount store," he told Boris.

McCracken, dressed as Superman, greeted Thurston and Natalie at the front door.

"Always thought you had a Sherlock Holmes complex," he told Thurston.

"What does that say about you, Superman?"

Thurston introduced his companion. "Irene Adler, meet Superman."

"Do you really have amazing powers?" Natalie asked.

"Yes, and no. I do, but I dare not use them. My wife Emily is over there." He nodded towards a woman wearing an outfit that looked like a large chunk of green matter. "She's kryptonite. The only thing that can kill Superman. When I start feeling too good, she brings me crashing down to earth. After all, why should tonight be any different than any other night?"

Natalie navigated over towards the cider bowl as Thurston surveyed the other guests. "Didn't know Winston would be here."

"We invited him," McCracken said. "Didn't think he'd come. He arrived with Audrey a few minutes ago."

Winston was dressed as a devil, his wife as a witch.

Anna Benson sidled up, hard cider in hand. She was dressed as a matronly, somewhat overweight woman.

"I give up, Benson," said Thurston. "What's different tonight? You look just the same."

"I came as Mamie Eisenhower."

"Really? I haven't seen many Mamie Eisenhowers at Halloween parties."

"Actually, there's another one over there by the barrel dunking for apples."

Thurston downed a glass of cider, then settled into an armchair in the living room near McCracken. Winston, cider in hand, wandered over and joined them.

"Well, if it isn't the devil," Thurston said.

"Who are you supposed to be?"

"Sherlock Holmes, of course."

"Shouldn't you have a pipe or a hat or something?"

"Lost them a half hour ago. I think Benson stole them.... What enticed you to leave the corridors of power to return to campus? McCracken's party?"

"No. The seminar I teach in microeconomics. Can't let my assistant run it every week."

"So what's going down in Washington?" asked McCracken. "Any scandals we should know about?"

"Nothing that exciting. I'm simply helping the Powers That Be smooth over some bumps in the road that cropped up over the last few years."

Thurston raised an eyebrow. "Bumps like tax policies that make the rich richer and the poor poorer? Bumps like how to keep the poor afloat when you're spending billions on a missile defense system you don't need?"

"No, Thurston. Bumps like inflation and small rises in unemployment."

"You've got a nice little racket going," Thurston told Winston. "You're advising the Powers That Be in Washington because you agree with their politics and they think you've got some clout here on campus. The only reason you have clout on campus is because you're advising policy makers in Washington, and that gives you a boost in your academic career. It's a vicious circle, and neither side realizes you don't know what the hell you're talking about."

"The same formula that worked for you when Carter was in power."

"Exactly."

"Don't let it get you down, Thurston. It's the way the game is played. You had your moment in the sun. Now you're sitting on the bench with the other has-beens."

"I beg your pardon," mumbled McCracken.

"Present company excepted, of course."

Winston emptied the glass of cider and finished off a donut. "Well, this has been fascinating, but I'd better move along. I believe I noticed Dean Pensky over by the mistletoe."

"There's no mistletoe," McCracken said. "This isn't a Christmas party."

"Apparently one of the guests brought along mistletoe to liven things up. Obviously been to your parties before."

As Winston maneuvered his way through the noisy crowd, Thurston asked McCracken if he had given more thought to seeking the department chairmanship.

"Other than telling the dean I'm available for the job, what can I do? I can't campaign for it. I can't put up 'vote for me' signs or hold rallies."

"You've got to be subtle. Half the professors in the department are waging subtle campaigns. You can be sure Winston is."

"Maybe I can advance my cause by letting the air out of Winston's balloon," McCracken said. "I'll be back in a minute."

McCracken fetched an envelope from his study. "Say what you will, Winston is a mover and shaker. This is the paper he prepared for a meeting in Washington next month. Has some interesting ideas on governmental regulation."

Thurston skimmed through it. "Amazing how his mind works. Like a garbage disposal. Collects a lot of random information and completely butchers it."

"Indeed. Too bad his pals in Washington will never see this."

"Why not?"

"When I noticed this on the desk in his office, I decided the policy-makers deserved better, so I wrote a new position paper advocating liberal views. Made a few copies and substituted my paper for his."

"So you think he will hand out your paper at the Washington meeting."

"I certainly hope so. Actually, I used his cover page on the first sheet. The rest of the paper consists of my ideas."

"You have a devious mind, McCracken."

"Thanks. It's nice to be appreciated. This should put a dent into his ambitions to be department chairman. ... Serves him right for criticizing my Halloween bash."

Nick and Boris found costumes at a Kmart, told an employee they wanted to try them on, and walked out of the store wearing their costumes and carrying their other clothes. A half hour later, they returned to the McCrackens' house. Nick was dressed as Frankenstein, Boris as Frankenstein's monster.

Nick fetched the box of papers he wanted to give Natalie from the back of the van and the two New Yorkers entered the house without being stopped.

"These are weird people," Boris said.

"Yeah," said Nick. "And somethin' tells me it's not because it's Halloween."

"What's in the box?" a man in surgeon's garb asked Nick.

"The monster's lunch," Nick replied. "A quart of your blood."

The surgeon gulped. "Scuse me. I think I saw a friend over there."

"I like this kind of party," Nick told Boris. "I can say anything and get away with it."

He noticed Natalie talking to Mamie Eisenhower and approached them. Boris wandered over to engage in small talk with Winston's wife, the witch.

"Nice party," Nick told Natalie.

"What are *you* doing here?"

"Someone forgot to invite me. Came anyway. We need to talk. Got message for you."

Carrying the box, he led her into McCracken's study. "I saw you makin' out with Thurston. You're supposed to be working, not fooling around! Moscow won't like this."

"Then don't tell them."

"Got to tell them. If project fails, I'll throw blame on you. More stuff I tell them about you, better I look."

"Wishful thinking, Nick. It will take a lot more than that to save your ass if things go bad."

He grimaced. "I know."

"I was told to get Thursty to cooperate. That's what I did."

"Thursty? You call professor Thursty?"

"Get over it, Nick. What's the message? Why didn't you use Jefferson's wheel cipher to encode it and just leave it for me?"

He shrugged. "I threw cipher away. By time I figure out how to code message, Cold War will be over. Don't know what Jefferson was thinking when he came up with that idea. Didn't have teevee in those days so I guess he sat around Monticello picking his nose and inventing things. ... Anyway, I decided to give you message in person."

"Well? What is it?"

"In this box is last part of economic data. K.G.B. says they must have book fast! Things falling apart. No need for someone to bomb Soviet Union, our fearless leaders are doing good job of destroying it themselves."

"Is that what you told Gorby?"

"Don't call him Gorby! His name is Gorbachev. Did I tell him he is destroying Soviet Union? Do I look stupid?"

"Oh, Nick, you've got to quit giving me openings like that."

"Why you say things like that? You're supposed to respect me. Fear me. ... I should have Boris slap you around. See if it helps your attitude."

"You're so stone-age, Nick. Times have changed. You need to change!"

"I like old times just fine. Don't want to change. What you see is what you get."

"That's sad."

"Yeah, well, stop screwing around with professor and finish project or we'll both be shipped to Moscow!"

"All right, Victor. Message received."

"Why you call me Victor? I'm Frankenstein."

"Victor was Frankenstein's first name."

"Well, call me Frank."

"Get out of here before you cause problems, Frank!"

"I came long way. Will leave when I'm ready!"

As they rejoined the crowd, Nick noticed something on the dining room table. "Is that pumpkin pie? I love pumpkin pie."

Natalie handed him the a paper plate bearing a piece of pie and pushed him toward the front door.

"All right, I'm leaving. Just get it done! ... Hmm. Pie is good, but needs whipped creme on top. Got any whipped creme?"

"Goodbye, Nick!"

He noticed Boris was talking to a vampire. "Let's go, Boris! She's not interested in you. She wants your blood!"

From his chair in the living room, McCracken saw that Frankenstein and the monster were leaving.

"Who was that? Didn't look like anyone I invited."

"I don't know," Thurston said. "Do you want Sherlock Holmes to check it out?"

"Don't bother. Half the people here probably wandered in off the street."

Near the end of the McCrackens' bash, Natalie glanced out a window and noticed a headless horseman riding down the street on his mount. His costume covered his head, making it seem that he was indeed headless.

"I see you, Natalie! You've got to come back to me!" he yelled.

It was Harry.

"I need you, Natalie, and — "

That was all Harry managed to say before the horse carried him directly under a large branch. The branch knocked Harry off the horse.

"Idiot," muttered Natalie.

A policeman wandered over to get Harry to his feet. Natalie was not sure if it was a real policeman or one of the guests. The policeman helped Harry into a van and drove off. If it wasn't a real policeman, she might have witnessed a kidnapping. Or, perhaps it was simply a pervert who planned to spend the evening with Harry.

Natalie returned to the party.

"Having an interesting time?" asked Thurston.

"You could say that," Natalie replied. "I'm feeling good. Someone spiked the cider."

"That would be *me*," said Superman, alias McCracken. "Care for another glass?"

13

November

THE FIRST SNOW OF THE season descended on Charlottes-ville on a chilly and windy Wednesday morning. Thurston was in a grumpy mood as he parked his Mercury and hiked over icy sidewalks to Monroe Hall. When he was younger, he didn't mind snow and ice so much, but now his body rebelled as winter drew closer. Late nights of working on the manuscript and making love to Natalie were taking their toll, too. He considered it a miracle that he managed to show up at the university for nearly all his classes and seminars. Of course, it helped that most of them were afternoon sessions.

He dropped his coat off in his office, then headed for the lecture hall.

"Morning, Benson," he mumbled as his nemesis, decked out in a dowdy brown coat and frumpy hat, shuffled toward her office.

She nodded. "You look like a train ran over you, Thurston."

"Late-night carousing is catching up with me. I think I'll give it up and spend my evenings watching the boob tube and kicking the cat around, like you do."

She glared. "You know, Thurston, if I become department chairman, your future here will be very bleak."

"I have tenure. You can't fire me without cause. The only way you could pull it off would be if I murdered the dean and you found the body *and* the gun in my house."

"I would hate to lose the dean," she conceded, "but if it would get rid of you, it might be worth it."

AS THURSTON STRODE toward the lectern in the lecture hall, he discovered Natalie was not in her seat. She had probably noticed the snow and decided to sleep a little later. Did she really think he would give her a passing grade simply because they were lovers? His morals were shaky, but he had to draw the line somewhere. Besides, if *he* had to be in class, so did Natalie. Before the session began, he ducked into an empty office down the hall and called her.

"Get out of bed and get over here! You're late!"

"Lord. You're worse than my mother ever was."

Thurston and his students were halfway through his class— "Beyond Statistics—How Economic Policy Affects People"— when Natalie slipped into her seat. Thurston scrutinized the seating chart, pretending he was trying to identify the late-comer.

"Miss Kramer, do you suppose you could try to be on time?"

"Sorry. I thought this was the day I go to Professor Winston's seminar on microeconomics. I figured I could skip it without missing anything important."

"Understandable. But in *this* class, you might actually learn something. ... Now where was I? Oh, yes. Economists and policy makers look at numbers for the gross national product, and unemployment, and new home construction, but most of the time they don't see the people behind the numbers. And in the last decade, they have essentially ignored those who are in poverty and the lower income levels. Under Kennedy and Johnson, there was much talk about helping the poor and helping them get out of poverty. The last decade, politicians have focused their rhetoric on the middle class. For example .... uh, Miss Kramer are we boring you?"

"Uh, I wasn't sleeping. I was thinking with my eyes closed."

"I see. Try thinking with your eyes open, will you? Then I can at least pretend that you're paying attention."

LATE THAT AFTERNOON, Thurston drove through slippery streets to Natalie's apartment, where he now passed most of his time. He could not ask Natalie to move into his house because his neighbors were incorrigible gossips who would spread rumors around campus that Professor Thurston had "shacked up" with a graduate student, setting off all sorts of repercussions within the Economics Department. In Natalie's neighborhood, nobody paid much attention to who was coming and going.

When he arrived at her apartment, Natalie was sprawled in a chair, editing a chapter they had written the week before.

"You embarrassed me in class," she said.

"Don't be mad. It was the most fun I had all day."

She set her work aside and kissed him on the cheek. "Maybe I should write a different book. An exposé about professors who screw their graduate students."

"You haven't got time. We've got to finish this one. ... What's for dinner?"

"I'm having a pizza delivered. Between working on the book and attending class, I didn't have time to cook."

"Hmm. Natalie's revenge."

"You'll think so after you eat it. I ordered a deluxe, heavy on the pepperoni, green pepper and anchovies. You'll be up all night with indigestion."

"Wonderful."

After they finished off the pizza, Natalie resumed editing the manuscript and Thurston browsed through economic data relating to the next chapter of the book.

"In a way, studying the Soviet economy is fascinating," he said. "It's like a laboratory experiment, Little rats running around in a cage, trying to revive an ailing economy. ... I'm reminded of a joke. How many Russians does it take to change a light bulb?"

"Enlighten me."

"None. They can't change it because they ran out of light bulbs last year."

Natalie shook her head. "That's terrible."

"Hey, don't blame me. I'm not making this stuff up."

"You aren't?"

"Okay. So maybe I am. ... I'm surprised the Soviet economy lasted this long, All this data suggests they're in much bigger trouble than people in this country or their own country suspect. I would say the situation is desperate. The data also dispels some of the myths about their economy that are prevalent in this country. It wasn't Reagan's posturing about stockpiling weapons or building a star wars defense system that brought about the collapse of their economy—it self-destructed on its own. And Gorbachev has been trying to save the Soviet economy by changing it rather radically, but his reforms actually are hastening the collapse. You'd think someone would have the balls to tell Gorbachev he's up a creek without a paddle."

"If you were in charge, how would you turn the economy around?"

"It's a little late for that. I'd fold up my tent and start over with a free market system. ... Could I have another piece of carrot cake?"

"Only if you don't embarrass me in class anymore."

"Sorry. No promises."

"You can be a real pain in the ass."

"That's what Cynthia said before she left me."

"I think I would have liked Cynthia."

"Nonsense. Nobody liked Cynthia."

Thurston got up and hurried toward the bathroom.

"What's the rush?"

"I feel diarrhea coming on. I think Natalie's Revenge has kicked in."

"It doesn't pay to mess with the maestro," she said playfully.

Thurston fell asleep. Natalie poured herself a cup of coffee and stretched out on the sofa. The stress of it all was getting to her. Working as an agent for the Soviet Union. Trying to write a book with Thurston while keeping him from discovering who he was really writing the book for. Nick traveling to Charlottesville, threatening to do terrible things to her. And Harry ... he still phoned three times a day pleading for her to let him back into her life and threatening to do violent things if she didn't. It was too much.

She decided to put her plan to get rid of Nick and Harry into motion. After all, it seemed like a win-win situation for her, no matter what happened.

IN THE MORNING, THURSTON left the apartment and drove to the university. An hour later, Harry called.

Natalie said, "Oh, it's you ... *Nick, will you be quiet? Harry is on the phone!*"

"Nick?" Harry repeated. "That's your boyfriend's name? Nick?"

"No, you heard me wrong. Nobody's here but me. ... *Nick, will you stop it? ... On second thought, don't stop it!*"

"That's enough!" Harry said. "I'm going to teach Nick a lesson. Then maybe you'll respect me."

"Good luck. He's going back to Brooklyn in about five minutes and you'll never find him! ... *Be quiet, Nick. I didn't tell him you work at Billy D's Auto Repair. He doesn't know where you work!"*

"Billy D's? In Brooklyn?"

"No, Harry. You heard me wrong ..."

But Harry had hung up.

14

IN THE NATION'S CAPITOL, threatening clouds hung overhead as Herbert Winston joined other prominent economists in the Old Executive Office Building adjacent to the White House for a meeting with the President's Council of Economic Advisers. The Council consisted of only three members, but a dozen senior and staff economists assisted the Council as it worked on policy recommendations. The Council also solicited input from other distinguished economists, such as Winston and nine other academics who had gathered on this particular Thursday.

"Winston! How are things in Virginia?" asked Dr. Jonas Willings, the Council chairman, who was on leave from Yale University.

"The infidels are at the gate. The free market is again under attack."

"Do what we did," Carl Bedrow, a University of Chicago professor, suggested. "Lock the doors and throw away the keys so they can't get in."

"You don't advance economics by closing the door to new ideas," said Thomas Wedgeworth, a University of California economist.

"What new ideas?" grumbled David Ridgeway, an M.I.T. professor. "There hasn't been a new idea in economics since Adam Smith wrote *The Wealth of Nations.*"

"All right. Who took the jelly donut?" demanded Willings.

"I did," said Bedrow. "Law of supply and demand. There was only one left. Deal with it."

The Council and the academic economists took their seats. Over the next hour, the group discussed the usual issues—unemployment, tax cuts, inflation, the need for more jelly donuts at their sessions. Then, Willings noted that Professor Winston had prepared a presentation.

"Thank you, Dr. Willings," said Winston. He passed out copies of the paper. "I have tried to offer new perspectives on governmental regulation."

Winston noticed several of the economists in attendance seemed to look at the handouts incredulously.

"You say these are your thoughts on the matter?" asked Bedrow.

"Yes. I tried to distill them so they would be succinct and to the point."

"I can see that," noted Dr. Willings. "I didn't realize you favored more restrictions on utilities."

"And mergers and takeovers," added Professor Wedgeworth.

"What?" Winston exclaimed. "I favor no such thing!"

He skimmed through a copy of the presentation he had
just handed out. "What the hell is this?"

"Don't you know? You just gave it to us."

"Gentlemen, I ask your indulgence. Obviously someone
has tampered with my presentation."

Wedgeworth said, "Well, since we have the thing, let's
see if these ideas have any merit."

"No! You don't want to do that!" pleaded Winston, but
his fellow economists were already skimming through the
presentation.

As Winston frantically placed a call to his secretary to
ask her to fax a copy of the original presentation, the economists in attendance discussed the ideas McCracken had
incorporated into his rewrite of Winston's paper.

Winston was livid as he rode back to the Pierpoint Hotel
in a taxi. Someone was sabotaging his efforts to be the next
department chairman. He was sure it had to be Thurston or
McCracken. He had other enemies in the department, but
they were harmless compared to those two troublemakers.
He was determined to find a way to disgrace Thurston and
McCracken. Permanently.

15

IN BROOKLYN, NICK Boorstin tinkered with the brakes on a Jeep that belonged to a businessman from the Bronx. A husky young man with unruly blond hair approached.

"Are you Nick?"

Nick scooted out from under the Jeep.

"I am Vladimir. Why you want to see Nick?"

"He's been fooling around with my girlfriend, Natalie."

"Are you crazy? I'm not fooling around with Natalie."

"So you *are* Nick. Well, pal, don't bother denying you're fooling around with Natalie. I know it's true. You traveled all the way to Virginia to see her!"

Nick got up and wiped off his hands. "It was business,

jerk ball. Just business. ... Why you bother me? You want to bug somebody, bug Thurston. Natalie and Thurston have something going."

"Who's Thurston?"

"Her professor boyfriend."

"*I'm* her boyfriend. Harry."

"She does get around. In Russia, we have name for women like that."

"Don't insult Natalie!" Harry growled. He drew closer and threw a punch at Nick. Nick ducked.

"You don't want to do that, cowboy," Nick warned.

"Yes, I do!"

Harry threw another punch. Before it could land, Nick belted him in the stomach. Harry doubled over and gasped for breath.

Nick turned to leave, but Harry grabbed him. Nick punched him again. Harry fell to the ground. Out cold.

Nick called Boris. "Come on over. Got a little mess for you to clean up."

Fifteen minutes later, Boris pulled up in his van, brakes squealing.

"Bring van in tomorrow," Nick said. "I'll fix brakes. Is my specialty."

Boris hesitated. He had heard about what happened to people after Nick had fixed their brakes. "No, that's all right boss. They just squeal a little."

"It's no problem. Bring it in tomorrow!"

"All right. ... What should I do with this guy?"

"Take away his cash, credit cards, IDs. Haul him to

police station. When no one is looking, pour vodka on him, smash the hell out of a police car and leave him there. They'll take care of him for us."

"Sure thing, boss. Sounds better than the last time."

The last time Nick had asked Boris to get rid of somebody, he had Boris put the body in a box and Boris mailed it to Russia. Unfortunately, the box never made it. Insufficient postage.

16

A FEW DAYS LATER, about a hundred students and faculty members showed up at an auditorium in Monroe Hall to hear Professors Eugene Thurston, Glen McCracken and Anna Benson discuss "Values, Ideology and Economic Policy". It was the third in a series of discussions sponsored by the Economics Department. McCracken was there because a good performance would earn him brownie points as the search for a new department chairman continued. Thurston was there because McCracken threatened to plant an item about his lovemaking sessions with Natalie in the Economics Department newsletter if he didn't show up. Benson was there because she had nothing better to do.

"In my view, one of the biggest problems in our profession involves the assumptions we make when we set out to work on a problem," McCracken declared. "If the assumptions are biased or flawed, the conclusions will be flawed. We need to take a good look at the way research is constructed. Then, when the research is finished, we need to make sure that our efforts to draw conclusions from the research are not biased by ideology or preconceptions. This can be a real problem because some economists are so welded to one part of the political spectrum or another, or so devoted to one economic theory or another, that they have trouble seeing things objectively. And the fact that much research is supported by organizations or foundations with their own agenda complicates things even further."

"Yes," agreed Benson, "but the other side of the coin is that values have a legitimate place in economics and economic theory. Economist A may say economists should only be concerned with productivity and inflation. Economist B says government has a responsibility to make life better for its people. Economist's A position is as much a value judgment as Economist's B's stand is. There are legitimate and varying points of view about the role government and the economy play in the life of the nation."

"What about the role of ideology in economics?" McCracken asked Thurston.

Thurston, who had been on the verge of falling asleep, paused a moment before answering. "An economist who is a slave to ideology is like a small-town boy who's never been to the big city. He has no idea what the world is really like."

"Care to elaborate on that?" Benson asked.

"No," muttered Thurston.

AFTER THE DISCUSSION, Benson drove herself home and Thurston and McCracken stopped by the Hungry Peasant for milk and beer. They were discussing human anatomy—Natalie's, specifically—when Herbert Winston approached.

"You're in trouble now," Thurston told McCracken.

"Maybe not. He doesn't know I was the one who sand-bagged him."

"All right!" Winston snapped. "I want to know which one of you did it!"

"Did what?" Thurston asked innocently.

"You know what I'm talking about. Which one of you rewrote the paper I prepared for the Council of Economic Advisers?"

"Why, Herbert. Why would we do that?"

"To embarrass me!"

"You don't need any help for that," McCracken commented.

"You won't get away with it! I asked the attorney general to investigate."

"Really," said Thurston. "And is he going to do it?"

Winston grimaced. "I don't know. He was laughing so hard, it was hard to get a straight answer. I don't think he understands the seriousness of the matter."

"And what did the Council of Economic Advisers think?" inquired McCracken.

WInston sighed. "They thought two or three of the ideas in the presentation had merit. What the hell is the world coming to?"

"I've often wondered the same thing," said McCracken.

"Well, don't think you're going to get away with it. ... By the way, Thurston. Scuttlebutt around the department has it you're writing a book."

"Don't believe everything you hear, Herbert."

"It's not true?"

"Oh, it's true, all right. Just don't believe everything you hear."

"What's the subject matter?"

"The Soviet economy."

"Don't you think you should become familiar with our economy before you branch out?"

"Why? You know nothing about it and you're advising the president's economic council."

"Gene's co-author is an attractive graduate student," McCracken noted.

"Really? How did you manage that, Thurston?"

"Animal magnetism."

"She was probably desperate to get a passing grade in your class."

"Well, that too."

"How is *your* book coming along?" McCracken asked Winston.

"It's finished and in the hands of the publisher. Should be out soon. It's called *Power Economics*."

"Sounds like it should be stocked in hardware stores, not bookstores."

"The publisher has big hopes for it. I don't pretend to understand the vagaries of the publishing business. Hell, I haven't figured out what's going on in our Economics Department. ... Well, I'd like to stay and exchange meaningless gossip with you, but I've got to prepare another paper for the C.E.A."

"That's the Council of Economic Advisers, in case you aren't familiar with Washington lingo," Thurston told McCracken.

"Thanks, Gene. I would have been up all night trying to figure that out."

Winston continued: "They want me to elaborate on one of the ideas in your paper. I won't do it, of course. I'll just say they should disregard the idea because I was drunk out of my mind when I wrote it."

"Good idea," Thurston noted. "Someone will leak to the press that a Virginia professor was drunk out of his mind when he wrote a government policy paper, the *Cavalier Daily* will throw it on the front page, and after a week of torment and speculation the university will fire you."

Winston suddenly looked much sadder. "I suppose you're right. My life used to be a lot less complicated, back when I was stupid and simple-minded like you. Well, see you around."

Winston shuffled toward the exit.

"He undoubtedly figures *Power Economics* will boost his career and his bid to be department chairman," Thurston commented. "Personally, I don't think he's got what it takes to be our chairman."

"No. Such a shame," agreed McCracken.

17

THURSTON PLANNED TO have dinner with Natalie at the Mongolian Grill, a little hideaway a few miles outside of town. When he pulled up in front of Natalie's apartment house in his Mercury, she was waiting for him, bundled in a blue parka and smoking a cigarette.

A Pontiac suddenly drew near and a young man got out. His clothes were disheveled, and he was limping.

"What happened to you, Harry?" Natalie asked.

"What happened to me," he muttered. "That's a good question. I go to see your boyfriend Nick in Brooklyn to tell him to get lost. I try to beat him up, but he gets in a couple lucky punches and next thing I know one of Nick's pals throws me into a van. He takes me to a police station where he dumps me out, pours cheap vodka on me and beats the hell out of a police car. A cop finds me and assumes I did this to myself, attacking the cop car and dumping myself in front of the cop shop because I want to get my picture in the papers. The cops send me to a hospital for a couple days and then I'm back at the police station and they give me the third degree—who am I? Why did I smash up a police car? Am I wanted for murder in Tennessee?

"They take my fingerprints and tell me who I am, which is a good thing because at that point I'm not sure who the hell I am, and they charge me with public drunkenness and mutilating a police car. I call my dad back in Oklahoma and he sends me the money to post bail, which unfortunately he won't get back because I got the hell out of New York as fast as I could. Which I guess you're not supposed to do if you're out on bail. So now, I'm not only crippled, there are warrants out for my arrest in New York, Virginia and Tennessee."

"That's terrible, Harry."

"Yes it is. And Natalie, I can't shake the feeling that somehow this is all your fault." He turned his attention to the economist. "I didn't catch your name."

"Thurston. Eugene Thurston."

"Something tells me you are Natalie's new, if somewhat over the hill, boyfriend. Nick wasn't really your boyfriend, was he, Natalie?"

"No, Harry."

"So why did I go up to New York to confront Nick and get the hell knocked out of me?"

"Harry, I'd love to stay and chat, but we've got to be going."

"Sorry. How rude of me."

Natalie settled into the passenger side and Thurston drove off. "I take it from what Harry said that he is a former boyfriend of yours and you somehow set him up."

"I suppose you could say that."

"Do me a favor. If we break up, let's split on an amicable basis and forget all the weird stuff."

"Of course, Thursty."

18

December

IN MOSCOW, MIKHAIL Gorbachev flipped through paper-work in the back seat of his Zil limousine as his driver, Dmitri, narrowly missed mowing down a decrepit old woman crossing the street.

"Damn pedestrians," mumbled Dmitri.

"Be more careful," Gorbachev cautioned. Then he noticed Yuri Oglavisky, a Kremlin hardliner who had given him a lot of grief, crossing the road a hundred feet in front of them. "But you get an extra twenty rubles if you run down Oglavisky."

Dmitri hesitated. Was Gorbachev serious or was he joking? How was Dmitri supposed to know?

Dmitri kept his foot on the accelerator.

"Slow down! Can't you tell when I am joking, Dmitri?"

Dmitri took his foot off the gas pedal. "I've got to find another job," he muttered.

"Me, too," mumbled Gorbachev.

The Soviet leader browsed through a pile of reports on the state of the economy and he was stunned. The Gross National Product was falling fast. Inflation was skyrocketing—retail prices were up more than 100 percent in a year. Not only that, consumers were using the new freedoms Gorbachev had given them to express their outrage at the government. Things had gone from bad to worse.

When he arrived at his office in the Kremlin, he summoned Andrei.

"Our economy is disaster! Where is report from American economist?"

"Our agent and the economist are working on it, Mr. President!"

"Why taking so long?"

"Agent Boorstin reports our mole and professor are lovers."

"So while Soviet Union is collapsing, Americans are making love. Why couldn't be other way around? ... Situation is serious. Tell our people in America if I don't see report in *two weeks*, they will *all* suffer!"

"Yes, Mr. President."

"And you will, too!"

"But Mr. President. I have known you since we were in school together. We have worked together for years!"

"Yes. Would pain me to send you to prison to do twenty years hard labor, so I suggest you get me report!"

"Yes, Mr. President. ... May I ask what is your Plan B?"

"Plan B?"

"Yes. What is your backup plan in case the American's book does not make things better?"

"The book *is* Plan B," Gorbachev said.

"Crap," mumbled Andrei.

"Exactly," said Gorbachev. "Two weeks!"

19

THE NEXT DAY WAS A Saturday, so Nick Boorstin did not go to work. He shopped for groceries in Brooklyn and browsed around a used bookstore, where he flipped through the pages of several pornographic novels before buying a copy of Somerset Maugham's *Ashenden*, a collection of spy stories drawn from the novelist's adventures during the First World War.

When Nick returned to his apartment, he fixed himself a ham sandwich, retrieved a bottle of vodka from the refrigerator and settled into the armchair he had purchased from the Salvation Army. After reading *Ashenden* for two hours, Nick was in the mood for some intrigue of his own.

He slipped on a black tee shirt, jeans and black leather

jacket, descended the stairs, fetched his Chevy from a parking space down the street—damn, another parking ticket—and drove to the dead drop on 43rd Street in Manhattan where Moscow sometimes left communiqués for him. Hidden from street view and stashed behind a loose brick were a torn Snickers candy bar wrapper and two coded messages. Nick took the coded messages *and* the Snickers wrapper (just in case it contained a message, too. Moscow was desperate. Who knew what the K.G.B. would try next?).

Nick returned to his Chevy, intending to return home immediately, but before he had driven five blocks he started daydreaming about Molly, her inviting body—not particularly shapely but alluring enough to draw attention in Russia—and the stern but somehow affectionate way she had of saying "Get out before my husband comes home you greasy pig!" Minutes later, when the honking of car horns roused Nick from his reverie, he discovered he had taken a wrong turn and was cruising through the Holland Tunnel, bound for New Jersey.

Damn. He did not *want* to visit Jersey. The only people he knew in Jersey were pissed off at him for messing with their brakes. After cursing capitalistic highway planners and asking for directions three times, he finally arrived back in Brooklyn.

Safely inside his apartment, Nick bolted his door and retrieved his decoding book from under the dresser drawer. He laid the booty from the dead drop out on his small wooden dining room table.

He examined the Snickers wrapper. To the untrained eye, it seemed to be an ordinary candy bar wrapper, but one should never underestimate the cunning of the K.G.B.

Looks could be deceiving. Perhaps a coded message was buried in the nutritional information, or the list of ingredients. "Soy lecithin" looked particularly suspicious. Wasn't that the code name of a K.G.B. operative in Panama? A brilliant insight, Nick told himself. An ordinary agent would not have noticed that. Unfortunately, it had no relevance to the matter at hand. Nick tossed the wrapper into a waste basket.

He turned his attention to the two messages. Making sense of the first one required a little work. It was from someone in Iraq and was intended for an Iraqi operative in America. Something about a car bomb, collateral damage, that sort of thing. Well, some poor sap would never get his orders. Too bad. He ought to check his mail more often.

The second message was from Andrei in Moscow:

> Things are going crazy. Inflation is rampant.
> Deficit is spiraling. Beloved President wants
> book in his hands within two weeks or we
> will all be in deep shit. Send the book!

Terrific. In Moscow, being in deep shit meant just that—being in deep shit in a slave labor camp. Why didn't Gorbachev find a hobby so he wouldn't have so much free time on his hands? Something like a treadmill would be nice.

Nick knew he must pressure Natalie to finish the book immediately, but he was no longer comfortable using the capitalistic telephone system. Perhaps his phone or Natalie's had been bugged. It was obvious he must go to Virginia again.

As he glanced out the window at the neon sign over the

bar across the street, he noticed snow was falling. Terrific. He did not like to drive in snow. A few years earlier he had totaled an old Ford pickup during a snowstorm. Killed three chickens, wounded a cow and dislocated his own shoulder.

Besides, he was tired. He would have Boris drive him to Virginia. Nick could relax as Boris did the hard work. He called his countryman.

"Pick me up in a couple hours. We're going to take a trip."

20

THE NEXT DAY, NATALIE met Thurston for lunch at the Friendly Virginian, a small cafe near the University of Virginia campus. It was a quiet place, except after basketball or football games, or on weekends, when students flocked there to drink beer and boast about their sexual exploits, the tests they had flunked, or how much they had paid for their phony IDs.

Natalie ordered a taco salad, Thurston a pulled pork barbecue sandwich.

"I looked over the last box of data on the Soviet economy," Thurston said. "Who did you say gave you that stuff?"

"An acquaintance. His name is Nick."

"Nick? Harry thought you had a boyfriend named Nick."

"He was wrong. You know how screwed up Harry is."

"He's not exactly a poster boy for Mental Health. ... The data is very interesting. Did you know that In 1985 it cost more to buy a loaf of bread than a small car ... or perhaps I read that wrong."

"Are you talking about a *toy* car?"

"Maybe that's why it was so cheap. That puts a whole new slant on it. It would help if I could read Russian. Half the words on those papers aren't in my Russian-English dictionary."

He took the paperback out of his sport coat pocket and showed it to Natalie.

"*Poor Ivan's Dictionary*," she read. "Fifty thousand Russian words, thirty thousand English words. Doesn't that leave twenty thousand Russian words they didn't translate?"

"Apparently."

"Вы идиот."

"Don't be crude, Natalie. I don't know a lot of Russian but I do know when you're calling me an idiot."

As Thurston and Natalie discussed the Soviet economy and the Russian language, Herbert Winston ventured into the Friendly Virginian with Dean Freida Pensky of the College and Graduate School of Arts and Sciences. Winston had asked the dean to lunch as part of his campaign for the department chairmanship. Pensky was a short woman in her late forties who wore her auburn hair in a tight bun.

She had a lisp, a husband who couldn't find a job, and a sour disposition. It was rumored she had not smiled since 1974, when a pickup truck rolled over the begonias in her neighbor's yard.

Winston and Pensky seated themselves at a table near the entrance. As Winston glanced around the restaurant, he noticed Thurston having lunch with an attractive young woman. He recalled seeing the woman at McCracken's Halloween party and wondering who she was. Could that be the graduate student who was collaborating on a book with the infidel?

The wheels in Winston's brain started turning. If Thurston was having an affair with one of his graduate students, it could be scandalous—and it could give Winston leverage in his drive to be chairman of the Economics Department while at the same time disgracing Thurston.

There was no time to waste. The dean was right there in the same restaurant with Thurston and his paramour. It was the perfect moment to plant seeds of doubt in the dean's mind.

"I see Professor Thurston is here. Wonder who the woman is that he's dining with."

Dean Pensky glanced at the pair. "Could be his daughter, for all we know."

Of course, Winston thought. *And I'm the king of England.*

"Don't think he has a daughter," he commented.

Fifteen minutes later, Winston was finishing off a ham salad sandwich when he noticed Thurston's companion slipping on her coat. He realized he must make a decision that could make or break his career. Should he finish lunch with the dean who held his future in her hands and let the young woman walk out the door—perhaps losing his chance to nail Thurston to the wall? Or should he risk offending the dean by abandoning her and following the young woman?

The young woman was nearing the exit. Winston knew he had to make a decision quickly. He pushed back his chair. "I hate to eat and run, Dean Pensky, but I have an appointment with a student back in my office."

"Oh. Of course. Go ahead and leave. I can manage."

Winston slipped on his coat and followed Natalie outside, where she climbed into a Volvo. He hurried over to his Land Rover and followed her. His hunch about the affair between Natalie and Thurston had better pay off. He had deserted the dean in the middle of their lunch. Not only that, the dean was stuck with the bill for *his* lunch. Good Lord, what had he done?

As NATALIE LED WINSTON through the streets of Charlottesville, Winston realized he needed proof that she was having an improper relationship with Thurston. Without proof, he had nothing. But how could he prove it without stooping to the level of a peeping tom with a camera?

Natalie drove until she came to the Last Chance Motor Lodge on the outskirts of the city. She parked nearby. Winston pulled up in the distance.

What was she up to? She had just left Thurston, the man Winston assumed she was having an affair with. Was she having an affair with another man, too?

Winston watched as Natalie strode with quick, firm steps toward the bench in front of the motor lodge. A short, shabbily-dressed man stood next to the bench. As Natalie approached, the man slipped a note inside a copy of a newspaper, folded the paper and left it as inconspicuously as possible, as though he were nothing more than a litterer.

Natalie hurried toward the bench. Suddenly, a tall, dark-haired man wearing a suit and overcoat seemed to be heading toward the same bench. Natalie picked up her pace, but he was closer. She hurried, and was nearly running now. She reached for the newspaper ...

The man in the suit reached it first, and picked it up.

"Oh, hello," he said. "It seems we were both after the newspaper. Tell you what, I'll share it with you."

"No, I ..." Natalie mumbled.

Winston noticed the scruffy-looking man was watching all this from thirty feet away where a tree partially hid him. He seemed to be very nervous about what was happening.

"I just want to see the sports section," the man in the suit told Natalie. He reached for the second section of the newspaper. The piece of paper the scruffy-looking man had stuck inside the newspaper fell out. She reached for it, but the man in the suit was quicker.

"Well, what's this?" the man said, and he began to read the message. Immediately she snatched it out of his hands.

"I'm sorry, but ... it's a note from my boyfriend. He's shy. This is how he makes dates with me."

She was thinking fast, but she didn't know if the man was gullible enough to believe her.

"Over there, that's him," she said. She smiled and waved at Nick.

Nick cringed, obviously exasperated because she had called attention to him. He did not wave back. He tightened his coat collar around his neck and tried to hurry away as inconspicuously as possible. He would have made it, too, if he hadn't tripped over the collie an elderly woman was walking.

"Seems rather shy and uncoordinated," the men noted. "That's a handy little system you have. If I leave a note in the newspaper tomorrow, can I get a date with you?"

"I'm afraid not," Natalie said, tucking the note into her coat pocket. "Rupert is the jealous type."

"Shy, jealous and uncoordinated. What other attractive traits does Rupert have? Sounds like he could use a psychologist."

"Rupert *is* a psychologist."

And Natalie hurried away.

Herbert Winston pondered what he had witnessed. What was that all about? It seemed secretive and highly suspicious.

He wrote down Nick's license plate number and Natalie's, then called Rose Grayson, a neighbor who worked at the local F.B.I. office.

"Rose? Herbert Winston. How are you?"

"Your dog's barking keeps me up nights and I haven't had a decent sleep in three weeks. Other than that I'm fine."

"I'll see what I can do about the barking. I need a favor, Rose. Could you tell me who a couple license plates belong to?"

"We aren't supposed to do that for civilians, Herbert. This is the F.B.I. We investigate murders, scams, terrorism, conspiracies, that sort of thing. We can't waste time chasing down people who run traffic lights or piss on your rose bushes."

"This could be bigger than that. Help me out, and if it turns out to be something suspicious, I'll let you know."

"Why, Herbert. What have you been up to?"

"It's not me. It's the freaking halfwits I associate with."

"Give me the license numbers. I'll see what I can do."

A half hour later, Winston was walking past the Rotunda when Rose called back.

"The first plate belongs to Nicholas Boorstin, a Russian immigrant. Works at at an automobile repair shop in Brooklyn. The other plate belongs to Natalie Kramer, a graduate student at the university."

"Russian? This thing is bigger than I thought! Let me talk to one of the agents."

"Are you sure you want to do that, Herbert? They don't like it when people waste their time."

"This might involve espionage or national security. Is that important enough for you?"

"All right, Herbert. I hope you're not just spittin' into the wind. And don't forget the dog!"

A few minutes later, a man with a deep voice and a Southern accent came on the line. "This is Agent Bruce Hargrove."

"Herbert Winston. Did Rose tell you why I'm calling?"

"Said you were a nut case who lived in the house next to hers."

"I live next to her. That part is right. Now look, Hargrove, I saw something very strange going down today and I knew you'd want to know about it."

"And what would that be, Winston?"

"I'm a professor in the Economics Department at the university. One of the other professors in our department, Eugene Thurston, is collaborating on a book with a graduate student. The book is about the Soviet economy. This afternoon, I followed the graduate student—"

"Why did you do that?"

"I wanted to find out if she and Thurston were having an affair."

"You're a peeping tom?"

"No, you idiot. I told you—I'm a professor at the university."

"Professors can be peeping toms. Just last year I handled a case—"

"Do you want to hear what I have to say or are you going to ramble on about meaningless trivia?"

"You're a professor all right. So what's going on, Winston?"

"I followed this young woman to the Last Chance Motor Lodge where she was covertly given a message by a Russian named Nicholas Boorstin, who lives in Brooklyn. I knew this was something you would want to look into."

"What did the message say?"

"How do I know? I just saw him leave it inside a newspaper on a bench and she picked it up."

"They could be lovers passing messages back and forth."

"She's a sophisticated woman. He looks like a rummy from the rescue mission. ... Look, Hargrove, for all we know this could have something to do with the Soviet Union and national security. You're going to feel awfully stupid if it comes out later you ignored a Soviet espionage ring. Will you look into it?"

"I suppose I've got to. ... Give me your phone number."

AS BORIS DROVE NICK back to Brooklyn, Nick was upset about the confusion at the drop. He consoled himself with the knowledge that in the spy game, things often went wrong. He recalled reading in a biography by Henry Zeiger, *Ian Fleming: The Spy Who Came In With the Gold*, that the British endeavored to help clear the way for the American invasion of North Africa by arranging for a tea merchant to prepare a leaflet, in Arabic, describing the virtues of Allied rule. The Royal Air Force dropped millions of the leaflets. Only later did the British learn the leaflet actually said, "Buy Mohammed Ali's green tea".

21

ON THE FRIDAY BEFORE Christmas, students and faculty participated in an annual ritual that was an integral part of university life: fleeing the campus and flocking to their cars, the airport or the bus station for the beginning of Christmas vacation.

As Thurston viewed the spectacle from the bar in the Hungry Peasant, it occurred to him the exodus resembled something he had seen in disaster films: masses of humanity desperately scrambling to leave town before the hurricane came ashore.

Thurston was envious. He wanted to be part of the fleeing horde of humanity. He wanted to get away from the university for a few days. He needed a break as much as those in the thundering herd did. And he would have been with them if it weren't for Natalie. She was such a workaholic. She had no interest in setting the manuscript aside for a few days and joining the fleeing masses. What was her problem, anyway?

He wistfully sipped his brandy, then drove home, being careful not to barrel into any of the fleeing faculty and students. Not that he didn't want to.

OVER THE WEEKEND, Natalie and Thurston worked on the manuscript for a few hours each day. Monday morning he drove over to his office at the university to check his mail.

As he passed Peabody Hall, he muttered to himself ... *he had reached his limit, he was only human, if he read one more report on inflation in Siberia he would explode.*

Glen McCracken came up from behind and joined Thurston on his journey to Monroe Hall. "Mumbling to yourself again, Gene. Not a good sign. You know people are already talking about you."

"What are they saying?"

"I don't know. They mumble, too. Or do you suppose my hearing is getting worse?"

"Could be. You aren't getting any younger, you know."

"Hmph. ... How are things with you and Little Miss I-Want-You-to-Write-My-Term-Papers-For-Me."

"She's fine. I wish she wasn't such a damn workaholic. I need time off to recharge my batteries."

As they entered Monroe Hall, McCracken said, "Why don't you simply tell her you need a vacation? Put your foot down! You've earned it. You don't need her permission to take a vacation!"

"Of course I don't. That's a good idea. ... Where are *you* going for Christmas?"

McCracken sighed. "Emily and I are staying here. If you ever feel the urge to get married again, Gene, read the fine print before you agree to anything. Especially the parts about taking vacations and till death do we part."

Two letters from publishers had been stuffed into Thurston's mailbox. Preston House declared it had no inclination to publish a book on the Soviet economy ("the subject is about as fascinating as sewage treatment plants in Poland"), but Marcy Noble, an editor at Laughton & Miles, expressed interest in Thurston's outline of the book, and offered a modest $3,000 advance. Thurston stuffed the letter and the check into his pocket and decided to wait until the time was right to tell Natalie about the offer.

After replying to correspondence in his office, Thurston pushed his black leather chair back, propped his feet up on his oak desk and gazed out the window. What McCracken had said made sense. Thurston was tired, mentally and physically. Natalie was pushing herself and Thurston too hard to finish the manuscript. He needed a break. He didn't need Natalie's permission—he could take a break whenever he wanted. And what better time to do it than Christmas week?

He skimmed through the yellow pages, then called a travel agent, asking her to book two round-trip tickets to New York City and to make reservations at a hotel near the Theater District.

An hour later, as Thurston sent darts hurling mercilessly

toward a photo of Professor Anna Benson, his phone rang. The reservations were all set.

On his way out of his office, he noticed department chairman Yardley heading toward him. "We need to talk," Yardley said.

Thurston started towards Yardley's office.

"Not here," Yardley said. "Let's take a walk."

As they left Monroe Hall, Yardley said, "What have you been up to that would get the F.B.I. interested in you?"

"The F.B.I.? Nothing."

"An agent Hargrove was snooping around the department offices asking questions about you. He's a little man. Doesn't look very fit. Probably doesn't get out of his office much."

"Oh, Lord. That nincompoop Winston got upset because somebody played a practical joke on him and he reported it to the F.B.I. That's all. I can't believe they're actually wasting their time looking into it."

"He asked about a graduate student, too. Natalie Kramer."

"Miss Kramer? She doesn't know anything about it. Winston is way off base as usual."

"I hope so. I don't want the department involved in anything that could prove embarrassing."

"Then get rid of Winston. I know a couple people who would do it at a bargain price."

"Don't say things like that, Thurston! I've got enough problems!"

WHEN THURSTON RETURNED to Natalie's apartment and told her about the vacation he had organized, she was not pleased.

"Are you out of your mind, Thursty?"

He plopped his tired body down on the living room sofa. "But Natalie, we need a few days off. We're getting burned out. *I'm* getting burned out."

"We can't go away now. There's too much to do. What we're doing is important."

"A couple of days won't matter."

"Thursty, if you're burned out, we can make things easier on you by forgetting about the sex."

"I'd be more inclined to forget about the book." He took her in his arms. "Trust me. A little time off will be good for both of us."

She wanted to say she couldn't go because Gorbachev would be upset with her, but Thurston would wonder what the president of the Soviet Union had to do with whether they took a short vacation. She gave in. After all, she needed a break, too.

22

THE NEXT MORNING, three days before Christmas, Thurston and Natalie climbed into his Mercury and he drove eight miles north of Charlottesville to the Charlottesville-Albemarle Airport. He wondered why a black Dodge didn't pass him, but the driver apparently was in no hurry. Thurston parked in the long-term parking lot at the airport and noticed the Dodge did, too.

In the waiting area Thurston and Natalie exchanged small talk about the weather and the eccentricities of their fellow travelers. After a twenty-minute delay, they boarded a US Airways jet. The flight to New York would take less than two hours.

As the jet cruised over northern Virginia, Thurston mentioned he had some good news.

"Really, Thursty?" Natalie said warily. "Isn't this vacation enough good news for a while?"

"I've found a publisher for the book!"

She gasped for air. *"What?"*

"Yes!" He took the check and the letter from the publishing house out of his pocket. "And they gave us a three thousand dollar advance!"

Natalie turned pale. "A publisher? Thursty, we aren't ready for a publisher. The manuscript isn't even finished!" What would Nick say if he found out? What would Moscow say if its secret project was *published* in the United States? And Moscow would hate the title Thurston had chosen: *End of the Road: the Collapse of the Soviet Economy.* "Maybe we should hold off on this. Take a step back and give it more thought."

"We can't hold off. It's like McCracken said—if the other book you were talking about is published first, we might be up the proverbial creek without a paddle when we go shopping for a publisher. Publishing is highly competitive and unpredictable. We've got to take this offer before the publishing house changes its mind!"

"But Thursty, we shouldn't decide something as important as this on the spur of the moment. There are many things to consider. Let's think about it. Okay, Thursty?"

Winston sighed and shrugged his shoulders. He pulled a copy of *Virginia Business* out of the pouch hooked to the back of the seat in front of him and flipped through the magazine.

Five minutes later, Thurston said, "Did I mention Herbert Winston is writing a book? Calls it *Power Economics.* It's about how economists interact with Washington politicians. Probably thinks it's going to win him the department chairmanship."

"And that's a bad thing?"

"Depends. Would you say the end of the world as we know it is a bad thing?"

Natalie smiled. Thurston's nemesis Winston was a consultant for Washington power brokers. What would Thurston say if he knew *he* was a consultant for the Soviet Union's power brokers?

THE JET LANDED AT La Guardia Airport fifteen minutes late but Thurston and Natalie didn't mind. If they had driven to New York, they would have been on the road most of the day and would be fighting horrendous traffic.

Snow was falling and sidewalks were slick with patches of ice when a taxi whisked them to a Marriott hotel near the Theater District. In the back of the cab, they hammered out an agreement: Thurston would decide where they would have dinner. Natalie would decide where they would go after dinner.

After checking in at the Marriott and settling into their room, they taxied to 54th Street and the restaurant Thurston had picked out—Lanie's, a Vietnamese hangout.

"Looks enchanting," Natalie said. "Did the guidebook give it five stars?"

"The guidebook I bought was more down-to-earth," Thurston noted. "It gave Lanie's two dollar bills."

Rattan chairs and bamboo curtains graced the interior

of the restaurant. Their waitress was a young Vietnamese woman with a coy smile and a wedding ring on her finger.

Thurston struggled trying to make sense of the menu until Natalie pointed out that if he turned the menu over, he would find an English version.

"Yes, well, I knew that, but I was going to order in Vietnamese."

"You know how to speak Vietnamese?"

"Not a word."

After a few minutes of indecision, Thurston ordered a rice and beef dish, Natalie the ginger roasted duck.

As they waited for their food and Thurston leafed through a *New York Times* he had swiped from an adjoining table, Natalie cast a discriminating eye on Thurston. He seemed rather distinguished in his dark blue suit and white silk shirt. He was sometimes a bit pompous, but he was always caring and considerate towards her. She could tell that he enjoyed being with her, and she enjoyed being in his company.

That's when she had an unsettling thought. This wasn't just an assignment any more. Could it be that she was falling in love with him? After fooling around for years with the likes of Harry and an immature undergrad at Columbia known as Luke the Lush, she enjoyed being in the company of a caring, cultured, mature man.

"Story in here about Aspen, Colorado," he was saying. "Did I tell you about the time I plunged down Aspen Mountain without skis?"

Well, relatively cultured and mature.

"Actually, I had skis on when I started down the mountain. Lost them somewhere around the second bend. When a ski patrol found me I was wrapped around a tree babbling incoherently."

"Like you're doing now?" Natalie asked playfully.

Thurston grimaced. "Not exactly."

After dinner, as Natalie waited for Thurston to use the little boy's room, she noticed a pay telephone near the entrance. She dialed Nick's number, disguising her voice to make it sound deep and sexy and Russian.

"Nick? This is Olga. Remember me? When we broke up, in Moscow, I promised that one day I would come after you and do terrible things to you. Well, today is the day. I am in New York ... outside your apartment, watching you."

"Really? Well, I don't know who the hell you are, Olga, but if you're outside watching me, you have a lot of company. An idiot named Harry is hanging around out there again, and maybe a Russian or two, and a couple of guys who look like American agents."

"You live an exciting life, Nick."

"You don't know the half of it, lady. My apartment and my phones are probably bugged. The world is listening as we talk ... Well, what the hell, it's a slow night and I'm horny as hell. Come on up to my apartment and we'll discuss whatever it was I did to you, and maybe make love or something. I got nothing better to do."

"Good Lord, little man. Are you that desperate?"

"Yes, I am. ... Who did you say you were?"

As Natalie hung up, she heard a scream. A half minute later, Thurston returned to their table.

"You'd think they'd put little pictures of men and

women on the johns. They labeled them in Vietnamese and I went into the wrong one."

From the Vietnamese restaurant they took a taxi to the Helen Hayes Theatre, where they joined a packed audience at the Broadway show "Prelude to a Kiss". While Thurston and Natalie watched the show, Bruce Hargrove, who had followed them from Charlottesville, called the New York City office of the F.B.I. He identified himself and said he needed telephone records of calls made from Lanie's Restaurant that evening.

"Are you on a case, Hargrove, or is your wife cheating on you?"

"I'm on a case. Could be a matter of national security. Could be garbage. Too early to tell."

"All right. Tell me where you can be reached."

After the Broadway show, Thurston and Natalie stopped off for a nightcap, then returned to the hotel. The next afternoon, they taxied to La Guardia for the flight home.

AS THE JET CRUISED ABOVE the clouds, Natalie thoughts again focused on her relationship with Thurston. They might be able to have a good life together if she could convince Nick and Gorby to stop bothering her. But how could she do that? The Soviet Union and the K.G.B. would not take kindly to it if she told them she was quitting the spy game and wanted to be left alone. They would only leave her alone if they understood they had no other choice.

As a stewardess passed out processed steak and chicken dinners, Natalie decided on a course of action. She would write another manuscript. A shorter one, revealing full details about Nick and the spying operations in the United States he was running for Gorby. She would send a copy to Nick and warn him that if anything happened to her or Thurston, the document would be given to the F.B.I.—and the *New York Times* and *Washington Post*. The Soviet spying operations in the northeastern United States—and South Carolina—would be worthless.

Yes, she knew what she had to do.

When Thurston and Natalie arrived back in Charlottesville, somewhat refreshed from their short holiday, Natalie secretly started working on her exposé. While she was busy with that, Thurston finished the fourth chapter of *End of the Road*.

The next day Thurston mailed the first four chapters to Marcy Noble at Laughton & Miles, along with a note accepting her offer to publish the book. No matter that Natalie had not agreed to it. He was sure she eventually would see the wisdom of signing with a publisher sooner rather than later. After all, what harm could it do?

IV

Launching the Book

January-April 1991

23

AFTER HIS QUICK TRIP TO New York City, agent Bruce Hargrove considered his next move in his investigation of Herbert Winston's strange remarks about alleged espionage activities. Professor Thurston's and Natalie Kramer's trip to the Big Apple had seemed uneventful except for the call Kramer made from the pay phone in Lanie's restaurant. Telephone records revealed she had called the Russian, Nick Boorstin. There was one other thing that bothered Hargrove. Why had Thurston and Kramer dined in a Vietnamese restaurant? Why not an American restaurant? Noticing details like that, Hargrove mused, separated the ordinary agents from the F.B.I. elite.

He decided to continue surveillance on Thurston,

Kramer, Boorstin and Winston. In a few days, after he received his agents' reports, he would decide if he was justified in spending more time, money and manpower on the case.

AS NATALIE PUSHED ahead on her exposé of Nick and the Soviet espionage operations, the words gushed out of her mind and onto the typewriter page effortlessly, like water cascading over Niagara Falls. Writing the document was therapeutic. All the aggression and anger that had been bottled up inside her since Nick first threatened her and her mother erupted onto the printed page. That was evident from the adjectives she used when referring to Nick: neurotic, psychotic, paranoid, pathetic—endearing little descriptions like that. She could have gone on for another fifty pages, but she was simply trying to put the essential facts on paper. Anything more was icing on the cake.

She mailed a copy of her exposé to Nick on a Wednesday, enclosing a note saying she would give Nick and the K.G.B. the book they were waiting for, but then she wanted out, and if they caused her any trouble, or anything happened to her or Thurston, copies of the exposé would find their way into the hands of people who could blow the Soviet spying operations to kingdom come.

IN BROOKLYN TWO DAYS later, Nick returned to his apartment after a hard day's work sabotaging brakes at Billy D's. Two men in suits and Harry were parked outside the apartment building. Apparently Harry wanted revenge for the beating Nick and Boris had dealt out the first time. He obviously didn't know when to quit. The other two men tried to look inconspicuous, but in Nick's neighborhood, where dirty jeans wore the norm, their black suits stuck out like nuns at a prostitutes' convention. Besides, the *New York Post* one of the men was reading was two days old. Nick concluded the F.B.I. had camped out in front of his apartment.

Why were they there? Perhaps his neighbors had ratted on him after he called them "capitalist pigs" a few too many times. Or perhaps old lady Rigsby, the octogenarian who lived on the first floor, had seen Boris hanging around the front steps reading *Das Kapital* as he waited for Nick to show up.

Nick waved to the agents. They pretended not to see him.

The elevator was out of commission so Nick hiked up the stairs to the third floor. Outside his apartment he found a brown envelope. It was from Natalie. It wasn't heavy enough or big enough to hold the book manuscript. What was she mailing him?

Nick settled into a chair in his living room with Ivan by his side and began reading the document. He was outraged. Natalie was threatening to tell the world about Nick and her spying for the Soviet Union? She was threatening to expose the Soviet spying operations in the Northeast—and South Carolina? Was she nuts? She couldn't get away with that. Who did she think she was dealing with—some amateur working for a banana republic?

Nick picked up the phone. It would be a brief call because he figured his phone had been tapped. "Boris? ... Remember Harry? He's here again. Pick him up. We're going to take a trip."

Boris joined the small group of people watching Nick's apartment, and when Harry headed toward a diner for supper, Boris started his van. Boris drove several feet ahead of Harry, stopped the van, grabbed Harry and threw him inside.

Boris parked down a side street near Nick's apartment and waited until Nick showed up. Harry was in the back of the van, his mouth covered with tape and his hands bound with rope. The federal agents were about a hundred yards away, in front of the apartment building.

Nick shook his head. "You should've let it go, Harry. Revenge don't lead to anything good."

Harry struggled to get free but couldn't.

"Where to?" Boris asked.

"Virginia."

24

WHEN NICK POUNDED ON the door to Natalie's apartment the next evening, Thurston was sprawled out on her bed in a deep sleep. Natalie was lounging on the living room sofa in a nightgown and bathrobe, editing a chapter in the *End of the Road* manuscript.

"What are you doing here?" Natalie demanded.

Nick grabbed her and pulled her outside. She shivered because it was about twenty degrees. He led her over to the van, where Boris slid the side door open.

"Friend of yours wants to see you," Nick said.

"Harry!"

"Good guess. First try, too!"

"What are you up to Nick?"

"Want to show you what happens when you screw around with us."

Boris took out a pistol and pointed it at Harry's head.

"What are you trying to prove?" Natalie said. "Harry means nothing to me. Go ahead and shoot him!"

Harry's eyes opened wide. He struggled to plead his case with Natalie, but she couldn't understand a word he was saying.

"I told you, Nick. You mess with me and that document goes straight to the F.B.I. and the newspapers. You and your buddy Boris will be playing spin the bottle with the other lowlife in prison for the next forty years."

He grimaced. "You've got a foul mouth. Why you say things like that to me? .... Well, maybe you're right. I'll torture your mother to show you I mean business."

"She's dead, you nitwit. You're a little late!" Natalie was counting on Nick not knowing her mother was still alive and had moved to a cheap boarding house in Akron, Ohio, where she was harassing the other residents. "I told you I'd give you your damn book, so get out of here!"

Nick slammed the van with his first. "This is not how supposed to work. ... I should kill Harry and shoot off your legs just to teach you lesson!"

Harry's eyes opened wide.

"You can't win, Nick. I've got the winning hand. Don't push me!"

"Let's get out of here," Nick told Boris.

Boris nodded at Harry. "What about him?"

"No use hauling him back to New York. We passed police station on way into town. You know what to do."

The incident looked a little suspicious to Tony, the F.B.I. agent Hargrove had assigned to keep an eye on Natalie. He called Hargrove.

"The Russian grabbed Natalie, took her outside, pulled a gun and threatened to shoot some poor sap he had in the van. Apparently she talked him out of it and the van took off."

"Did you follow it?"

"No. You told me to watch Natalie and Thurston. Didn't you assign agents to watch the Russian?"

"Yes, but he eluded them. Let me know if anything else happens."

Natalie called her mother in Akron.

"About time I heard from you. Why don't you call more often?"

"I've been busy, mother. Do me a favor ... don't answer the phone for a few days. Let a friend answer. And if someone named Nick calls, have your friend tell him you're dead."

"What? ... *Dead? ... Why? ... What kind of trouble are you in now?*"

"You don't want to know, mother. Just tell him you're dead. ... Look, if Nick finds out you're *not* dead and threatens me, I may have to throw you to the wolves. If I tell him where you live, do you think you could survive a little torture? Dad always said you were a tough old bird."

"*What the hell are you talking about, Natalie?*"

"Oh, I'm just thinking out loud. Everything will be all

right. Just don't answer the phone, keep your doors locked and your bag packed."

"Natalie!"

"I'm joking, ma. Forget I said anything. I didn't mean to upset you."

"This has something to do with those commies you hung out with in college, doesn't it, Natalie? I tried to tell you that you were playing with fire and you were goin' to get burned. You never did listen to me. Why couldn't you be more like your brother?"

"I thought Tommy was in jail. For writing bad checks."

"He is. At least I know where he is. I don't worry about him. ... How come you never write? Would it kill you to write?"

"Got to go, mom. 'Bye."

The next day's *Charlottesville Mirror* reported United States planes had begun bombing runs over Iraq. Operation Desert Storm, aimed at forcing Iraq to pull its troops out of Kuwait, was under way. The beginning of the war was the big story on the front page, but on the local news page, a strange item attracted Natalie's attention:

MAN CHARGED
WITH ATTACKING
POLICE CAR

The story reported that 29-year-old Harry Ashley had been charged with public drunkenness and destruction of police property after being found unconscious, bruised and battered next to a damaged squad car in front of the police station. When taken into the station, Ashley was heard mumbling, "Natalie, Nick and Boris did this. I'm the *victim!*"

In late February, Harry was released from jail, just as President George Bush declared a cease-fire in the Persian Gulf War. Neither Harry nor Iraq was in very good shape.

25

March

As Thurston and Natalie scrambled to finish *End of the Road*, Marcy Noble, an editor at Laughton & Miles, called.

"We aren't there yet, Thurston."

"What are you talking about?"

"Your manuscript. I read the first four chapters. We aren't there yet. It's too academic. You've got to jazz it up. Make it interesting. Simpler. More exciting!"

"You understand we're talking about a book about the Soviet economy?"

"Right. But we're not there yet. Take chapter two, for example. You say, 'Beginning in 1928, a series of Five-Year Plans set goals for the Soviet economy. These economic goals were determined by the bureaucracy rather than market conditions.' And then you describe each of the five-year plans. Boring, Thurston. Get rid of that chapter and cut to the chase."

"Marcy, be reasonable. I can't write about the Soviet economy without discussing the five-year plans."

"Hmm. I disagree. Focus on the last five years. All that other stuff is ancient history. Bottom line, Thurston: Revise the book and deep-six the boring stuff. ... By the way, we've lined up a book tour for August. You might want to finish the manuscript or you won't have a book to sign. Eight cities, twelve days, twenty-one interviews."

"Crap. I planned on resting after I finished it."

"That's not how things are done, Thurston. After you finish writing the thing, the hard part begins. Selling it."

Thurston hung up.

"That was Marcy Noble. By the way, I accepted her offer to publish the book and kept the $3,000 check. I've got your half to give you."

Natalie stopped typing and glared at her co-author. "You're really complicating things, Thursty. ... Why did she call?"

"To tell me we aren't there yet."

"What does that mean?"

"She wants us to repackage the manuscript into something more marketable. Less informative."

"She wants us to mutilate it?" Natalie muttered.

"She used different words, but that's the idea. ... We probably don't have a choice since I spent a chunk of the advance already."

Natalie sighed. So not only would Moscow's book be published, it would be dumbed down. Nick and Moscow would be furious.

As Thurston began rewriting the first four chapters, Natalie decided there might be a way out of the mess they were in. She and Thurston would work on a new, racier version of the book for the publisher. She would hang on to the first draft and give it to Nick to send on to Moscow. If Nick heard about the published dumbed-down version, he might not realize it was the same book he had sent to Gorbachev and his buddies.

Over the next two days, Natalie made a few changes to the original manuscript and sent it to Nick. Perhaps that would get Nick and Moscow off her back.

IN BROOKLYN, NICK waited impatiently. Any day now Natalie would be leaving the manuscript at the dead drop. He just needed to know when. He waited for her call.

Then, one day when he arrived home from work, a package lay outside his apartment door. He picked it up and carried it into his apartment. It was postmarked Charlottesville. He tore open the packaging. Inside was the manuscript! The top-secret manuscript! She had sent it through the United States Postal Service! Any dummy could have torn it open and read it. And she had sent it regular mail. She didn't send it overnight! She didn't insure it! What was she thinking?

Nick leafed through the manuscript. As near as he could tell it seemed to be what Moscow wanted, but what the hell did he know?

He called Boris. "Got package to pick up. Take it to Rez-koff."

Niki Rezkoff worked at the Soviet embassy in Washington. It would take him about four days to get the package to Moscow by diplomatic courier. If he sent it by overnight international mail, it would get there much faster. But that was the way Moscow handled things.

And that attitude explained, Nick mused, how the Soviet Union had gotten itself into all that trouble in the first place.

OVER THE NEXT FEW days, Natalie and Thurston punched up the first four chapters of *End of the Road* with amusing anecdotes. When they finished, Natalie bundled up the pages and mailed them to Marcy Noble at Laughton & Miles.

26

April

THE ALARM CLOCK BLASTED Herbert Winston awake at 7 a.m. on a humid, rainy day and he reluctantly pulled himself out of bed.

"Morning already?" asked Audrey, his wife for the past twenty one years.

"Go back to sleep," Winston said.

No use getting her up. She didn't need to go anywhere and if she got out of bed to fix his breakfast, she would find something to argue about, starting his day on a depressing note. Yes, better if she slept in.

Winston showered, then fixed himself a breakfast of eggs over easy and toast. By 8:30, he was in his Land Rover enroute to the university to teach a 9 a.m. seminar in economic history.

As he passed Cabell Hall, he was worried and depressed. The Council of Economic Advisers no longer seemed interested in making use of his wisdom. He was sure it was because Thurston or McCracken had sabotaged the paper he had prepared for the Council. He had not told anyone at the university about his fall from grace in Washington; he still traveled there every three weeks or so because he wanted colleagues in the Economics Department to assume he was still a Washington insider. With the chairmanship of the Economics Department still up for grabs, he needed to use every weapon in his arsenal if he was to have a prayer of winning the job.

He hadn't heard anything back from agent Hargrove about the Russian and his connection to Natalie Kramer and Professor Thurston. What was the F.B.I. doing about it? Winston had done their job for them, digging up the information in the first place. What more did the F.B.I. need? Wasn't it obvious some sort of national security issue was involved? Or some sort of tawdry scandal? A blooming idiot could connect the dots.

Winston decided it was time to light a fire under Hargrove. He stopped off at his office on the way to class and called the F.B.I.

"Rose? Winston here. I need to talk—"

"Your dog is still keeping me awake at night. Why haven't you put him to sleep?"

"I never told you I'd put him to sleep. He's part of our family. If your cousin was causing the problem, would you put *him* to sleep?"

"If he barked all night? In a minute!"

"Look, I'll do something about it. Let me talk to Hargrove."

A short time later, Hargrove came on the line.

"Yes, Mr. Winston ..."

"What have you found out about Thurston, Kramer and Boorstin? I haven't heard from you!"

"Well, no sir. We aren't private detectives. We don't report to you. We work for the government."

"But *I'm* the one who told you about this. If I know what you're doing about it, I might be able to run down more information for you."

"Well, sir, we do have Nick Boorstin under surveillance. I can tell you that his actions have been suspicious. He has made several cryptic phone calls, and we were told he made a drop to someone in Charlottesville."

"*I* was the one who told you! Is that all you've got, Hargrove? What do you agents do all day? Bang Rose and the other secretaries? Pester the C.I.A. with crank calls?"

"Mr. Winston!"

"Sorry, I was out of line. I apologize."

"I should think so. ... Who told you?"

"What?"

"Just kidding, Winston. Lighten up a little."

"Our tax dollars at work. Look, Hargrove, when will you be finished with your investigation? I want you to accompany me to a meeting of the Economics Department faculty in two weeks to report on what you've found out. A new chairman is going to be appointed to head the department and all this could have a bearing on the decision."

"Let me check my schedule. ... Hmm ...I can delay my testimony before a grand jury and postpone torturing two mass murderers ..."

"What?"

"Still joking, Professor Winston. Actually, I expect to wrap up the investigation quickly, so I should be able to discuss our final report in two weeks. Don't worry. I will be there."

Winston rubbed his hands gleefully. When the department learned what Thurston had been up to, Thurston wouldn't have a prayer of being named chairman—nor would his pal McCracken, because McCracken's association with Thurston would doom him. And Winston would look like a hero for uncovering the espionage ring and asking the F.B.I. to investigate.

Herbert Winston, chairman of the Economics Department. Yes, he liked the sound of that. Everything was moving along smoothly. Nothing could be allowed to interfere.

He called home. "Audrey, we've got to get rid of the dog."

27

THE NEXT DAY, AGENT HARGROVE showed up at Monroe Hall and waited until Thurston finished delivering a class lecture. Then he followed Thurston to his office.

"Professor Thurston, I need to talk to you."

"My office hours are Tuesday mornings from three to four."

"I noticed that. I prefer to talk to you *now*." Hargrove flashed his identification. "Bruce Hargrove, F.B.I."

"Is this about that silly prank involving the paper Professor Winston presented to the Council of Economic Advisers?"

"I don't know anything about that," Hargrove said. "Should I?"

"No. It never happened."

Hargrove pulled up a chair. "Do you know a Miss Natalie Kramer?"

"Of course. Graduate student. She's in two of my classes."

"What is your relationship with Miss Kramer?"

"We're collaborating on a book."

"A book?"

"That's right."

"What is the book about?"

"The Soviet Union's economic problems."

Hargrove grimaced. "Do you know Nick Boorstin?"

"Never heard of him."

"We suspect Boorstin is engaging in espionage for the Soviet Union. And Natalie Kramer has been in contact with him."

"That's impossible. Natalie would never ... Oh, Lord. You say his name is Nick? She did mention that she got some of the economic data from a friend named Nick."

"To your knowledge, has Miss Kramer been engaged in passing information to the Soviets?"

"No. Just the opposite. In order to analyze the Soviet economy, we use data *from* the Soviet Union."

"Has she ever visited the Soviet Union?"

"I don't think so."

"Have you visited the Soviet Union?"

"No."

"Have you found a publisher for the book?"

"Yes."

"And it will be published in the United States?"

"Yes."

"It is puzzling," Hargrove conceded. "How could a

book that is going to be published in the United States be considered a result of Soviet Union espionage in the United States?"

"Exactly," said Thurston.

"Do you think Herbert Winston is involved in this in any way?"

"I wouldn't be surprised," said Thurston. "But *I* am not!"

CONCERNED ABOUT information that surfaced at his meeting with agent Hargrove, Thurston drove directly to Natalie's apartment.

"Hi, Thursty," Natalie said, as Thurston came in the door. She was wearing a bathrobe and her hair was wet. "You're home early."

He hung his coat in a closet. "An F.B.I. agent showed up at my office today. There are a few little things that I need to ask you about."

She swallowed hard. "Like what?"

"Such as what your connection is with Nick Boorstin. And the Soviet Union. And why you maneuvered me into writing a book about the Soviet economy. Little things like that."

"I can explain, Thursty. Really I can."

"Please do."

"Well, it's a long story." They sat on the sofa. She told him how she met Nick at Columbia University, how he trapped her in his web of international intrigue, and how he had contacted her before the school year began to give her the assignment from Moscow. "So, to make a long story short, they told me I had to convince you to collaborate with me on a book about the Soviet economy. The Soviets were in a real mess and they wanted your advice on what to do. The book we wrote was to be sent to them."

"So all the nights we spent together, working on the book and making love ..."

"It meant something, Thursty. Really. I love you."

"Must have scared the hell out of you when I found a publisher."

"It certainly did."

"I don't think they could nail you or me for spying since the book is being published and will be available in bookstores everywhere."

"I wouldn't think so."

"In a way, it was Moscow and Nick who brought us together."

"Yes. Thursty. And one more thing. I put everything I know about Nick and the Soviet espionage operations on paper, sent Nick a copy and told him if they don't leave me alone I'm going to give the paper to people who can expose their whole operation here."

"That must have angered him."

"Yes. But it convinced him to let us alone. Nobody got hurt but Harry."

"What happened to him this time?"

"About the same thing as last time."

He rose from the sofa. "Well, let me think about all this. When I met you, I didn't know I was getting involved with Mata Hari. ... It's probably best we don't see each other for a few days while I sort it all out."

"I love you, Thursty."

"I ... well, let me think about it."

28

THE NEXT DAY, AGENT Hargrove parked in front of the apartment house where Natalie lived and made his way to her apartment on the second floor. He knocked loudly.

"Natalie Kramer?"

"Yes," she answered cautiously.

"Bruce Hargrove. F.B.I. We need to talk."

He followed her into the living room, where she invited him to sit down.

"F.B.I.? That explains it. I was wondering who was sitting out front in a black Chrysler the last few days. I thought he was a well-dressed stalker who had an addiction to pizza. You might want to check his expense account. I think he had a prostitute delivered to his car the other night."

"Thanks for the information, but I believe that was agent

Vincent. She works for me, too. ... I need to ask you a few questions. Would you like to have an attorney present?"

"For you or me?"

Hargrove smiled. "For you."

"No."

"Miss Kramer, what is your relationship with Nick Boorstin?"

"I have known Nick since I was an undergraduate at Columbia University."

"Were you aware he was a Communist?"

"Yes."

"Since you met Nick, has he ever asked you to engage in espionage activities?"

She paused. "Yes."

"And did you?"

"I don't know if it could be considered espionage activities. He asked me to collaorate with Professor Thurston on a book analyzing weakneses in the Soviet economy. The information was to be sent to Moscow. However, Thurston has arranged for the information to be published in the United States, so I am not sure if that could be considered espionage."

She handed Hargrove a copy of the *Charlottesville Mirror* which contained a story reporting that the publishing house of Laughton & Miles would publish *End of the Road*.

"I see your point," said Hargrove. "Why did you agree to help Boorstin?"

"He threatened to kill me or my mother if I did not."

"You were an unwilling participant ..."

"Yes."

"What happened the other night, when Boorstin and his sidekick pulled up in a van outside?"

"Nick had taken Harry, an old boyfriend of mine, hostage and threatened to kill him because I had informed Nick that if he and Moscow didn't let me alone, I would expose his spying operations in the northeastern United States. And South Carolina."

"I see."

Natalie walked over to the desk where her typewriter sat and pulled a manuscript out of the drawer.

"This is the information. Everything I know about their operations in the United States."

Hargrove flipped through the pages. "Incredible. ... Thank you very much, Miss Kramer. Don't leave town until I get all this sorted out."

"Of course."

He headed toward the door, then paused. "Professor Thurston is a very lucky man."

Natalie smiled. "He doesn't think so. At the moment, he's not talking to me."

"Then he is a very stupid man."

"Yes, he is."

V

The End of the Ride

May-December 1991

29

May

NICK WAS ENGROSSED IN reading Graham Greene's *Our Man in Havana* when a news broadcast airing on the television in his living room penetrated his consciousness:

"In Moscow, consumers alarmed by steep price increases went on a buying frenzy for the third straight day. Tonight, Soviet President Mikhail Gorbachev addressed the Soviet people, telling them the shift to a market economy was necessary and imploring them not to panic."

Nick shook his head. It was a little late for that, Gorby.

"Next week, the predicament of the Soviet economy will be the topic of conversation on 'Book Explorer', when we interview Natalie Kramer and University of Virginia Professor Eugene Thurston about their new book, *End of the Road: The Collapse of the Soviet Economy."*

Nick stared at the screen. He must not have heard the announcer correctly. Then he noticed the announcer was holding up an advance copy of the book ... with Natalie's and Thurston's names plastered on the cover.

"What the hell is going on?" Nick mumbled. The manuscript the Soviet Union ordered produced in secrecy ... *it was being published in book form? In the United States? For everyone to see?*

Gorbachev would not be happy. Nick decided he might as well start packing. They would be coming for him soon.

In Moscow the next day, Mikhail Gorbachev summoned Andrei and asked about Project Economy.

"The good news," Andrei said, "is that we have received the book."

He handed the manuscript to Gorbachev.

Andrei's voice got lower as he continued. "The bad news is ... it's going to be pubished ... in book form ... in the United States."

"Speak up, Andrei. I did not hear you."

"I said ... it's going to be published. In book form. In the United States."

"What? Our secret book is going to be published? In America?"

"That is what our intelligence agencies report."

"Someone must pay for this! ... Do we have enough left in the budget to bring this Nick Boorstin and the woman ... what's her name? Natalie? ... back to Russia?"

"No, Mr. President."

"Or to have them knocked off in United States?"

"No, Mr. President."

"Helluva way to run a country. Well, we can't just sit around while Americans publish our secret projects. Tell Boorstin to stop publisher from releasing the book. Do whatever is necessary! This is top priority!"

"Yes, Mr. President."

30

THREE DAYS AFTER Thurston confronted Natalie about allegations of Soviet espionage he dropped by her apartment. She was preparing Chinese food.

"I see you're making spaghetti again."

She smiled. "It's what I do best."

He led her into the living room. "I thought about what you said. Maybe we should get a fresh start. No more lies. No more spying. Our relationship must be based on complete trust."

"I would like that." She extended a hand for him to shake. "Hello. I am Natalie Kramer."

"The name is Bond. James Bond." He took her in his

arms and kissed her. "The next phase of our lives may be pretty boring compared to the last few months."

Natalie played with his hair. "If that's what you think," she said, "you don't know me very well, Mr. Bond."

"Did that F.B.I. agent—Hargrove—come to see you?"

"Yes."

"Did he say anything about sending you—or me—to prison?"

"No."

"What did he say?"

"That you are a very stupid man."

"Any particular reason?"

"No."

"I don't think I like him."

"I do."

"You always did have a strange taste in men. Look at Harry."

"And you."

She kissed Thurston and he guided her into the bedroom.

"Why, Mr. Bond. What are you doing?"

"What I do best."

31

THE NEXT DAY NICK checked the drop site on 43rd Street and found a coded communiqué from Moscow. He was to use *any means necessary* to make sure the publishing house did not print Thurston's and Natalie's book. And he was to ship Gorbachev a case of those little chocolate mints he liked.

Nick called Boris on a pay phone. "Meet me. We got big job to do."

"Boss, I haven't been paid in months."

"I know. But Moscow will have us killed if we don't do this."

Boris picked up Nick in his van.

"We're going to blow up a publishing house," Nick announced.

"Sure thing," said Boris. "Thought you said F.B.I. was watching you."

"They're back watching my apartment. I snuck out the back door. ... Can you lay your hands on load of dynamite?"

"Sure. No sweat."

"Pick up *two* boxes. Might be big building."

The next evening, Boris rendezvoused with Nick again.

"You got dynamite?" asked Nick.

"You bet."

"Where?"

"Back seat and the trunk."

"Holy crap. Be careful driving. You hit bump, we could be blown to smithereens."

"Sure, boss. No sweat."

Boris pressed the accelerator and the van spurted from zero to fifty miles an hour in about seven seconds.

"Slow down, Boris!"

"Sure thing. Where we going?"

"Third Avenue. ... How did you get driver's license?"

"Driver's license? I need driver's license?"

As they approached the Laughton & Miles publishing house on Third Avenue, Nick told Boris to slow down.

The van kept going.

"Hit the brakes, Boris!"

"I'm trying," he growled. "Damn brakes won't work."

"Oh-oh," said Nick, who had worked on the brakes. The van kept rolling. "Bail out!"

Nick and Boris jumped out. The van cruised another hundred feet, then slammed into the side of a jewelry store. The van burst into flames. Seconds later, the dynamite exploded, sending flames high into the air.

"Holy crap," said Nick.

"Yeah," agreed Boris.

As people converged on the scene to watch, Nick and Boris hurried off—in the opposite direction.

Nick soon realized dynamiting the publishing house would not have stopped publication of the book anyway. The Third Avenue building was the home of the editorial offices. The book would actually be printed at a manufacturing plant in New Jersey.

32

June

END OF THE ROAD APPEARED in bookstores the next week. Nick worried about what Moscow might do to him in retaliation for letting the book be published. He also worried about the two F.B.I. agents still camped in front of his house. He feared they had connected him to the bombing of the jewelry store on Third Avenue. Or spying for the Soviet Union. Or kidnapping Harry.

In mid June, a loud knock on the door startled him. "Nick Boorstin, open up! F.B.I.!"

Nick opened the door slightly. The two F.B.I. agents barged in, threw Nick against a wall and handcuffed him.

"You are under arrest," said the taller man.

"Okay," Nick said.

"Don't you want to know the charges?"

"Not particularly."

The agents looked at each other questioningly. Then they yanked Nick toward the door.

"Turn off TV and lights," Nick said. "Don't want to run up electric bill."

Boris was arrested at his apartment in the Bronx. All told, seven people were taken into custody and charged with spying for the Soviet Union.

33

TWO HOURS AFTER THE arrests, Thurston and McCracken hiked across campus to attend a meeting of the Economics Department faculty at Monroe Hall.

"You'll be happy to know I am joining the ranks of book authors," McCracken said. "Instead of publishing a paper, I too am writing a book. I call it *All About Taxes*. It should be successful. After all, everybody talks about taxes. And there's so much misinformation about tax cuts and tax increases that—"

"That you decided to add to the misinformation."

"No! ... Well, I suppose so. But it should sell a few copies and earn me some respect in the department."

"It doesn't sound academic enough, You're dummying it down to sell more books."

"That's what the publisher wanted. What is your book called?"

"End of the Road: the Collapse of the Soviet Economy."

"Yes, I can see how you aimed that at the academic market instead of the mass market."

As Chairman Yardley bustled into the meeting room, Thurston said, "Professor McCracken is writing a book, too!"

"Who isn't," mumbled Yardley.

"So much for respect," McCracken said.

The eleven professors in attendance and the lone visitor seated themselves around the conference table.

Yardley reported the custodial staff was still having trouble with liquor being spilled near waste receptacles and someone was still stealing toilet paper and taking it home.

"My Lord, Anna," Thurston told Professor Benson. "You promised to stop pilfering the supplies!"

"I did no such thing!" Benson declared.

"You mean you didn't pilfer them, or you didn't agree to stop pilfering them?"

"Behave yourself, Thurston," cautioned Yardley.

McCracken moved his chair a little further away from Thurston's.

Yardley announced that the search for a new department chairperson was nearing an end. "We've narrowed it down to three candidates. A decision will be made in the near future."

Thurston mumbled, "After they've had a chance to shake down the candidates for more bribes."

McCracken carried his chair to the other side of the room and sat.

Yardley glared at Thurston. "And of course there are some professors who never were in the running for the job. ... Any more business?"

"Yes, there is," Winston asserted. "A matter has come to my attention that needs to be dealt with. It involves one of our faculty members. Professor Thurston."

"Me?" said Thurston. "What did I do?"

Winston nodded at the short man with close-cropped black hair sitting next to him. "This gentleman is agent Bruce Hargrove of the F.B.I. ... It came to my attention that Professor Thurston is writing a book—"

"That's against the law now?" asked Thurston.

"In your case, it should be," declared Benson.

Winston continued. "And he is collaborating on the book with a graduate student, Miss Natalie Kramer. I became concerned about this when I witnessed Miss Kramer rendezvousing with and apparently secretly receiving information from Nick Boorstin, who is a Russian immigrant living in New York City. I feared there was some sort of espionage going on—some sort of breach of national security—and I felt it was my duty to pass the information along to the F.B.I. Which is why Agent Hargrove is here. Agent Hargrove, will you tell us what you found out?"

"I am not at liberty to divulge sensitive information, but I want to correct what Mr. Winston said so innocent people are not falsely accused. Two hours ago, Nick Boorstin, his sidekick Boris and five other people were arrested for committing acts of espionage on behalf of the Soviet Union. The F.B.I. is satisfied that Miss Kramer and Professor Thurston did not commit any acts of espionage. We found no connection between Mr. Boorstin and Professor Thurston, and as for Miss Kramer, she was most helpful in breaking up the spy ring. Basically that closes the case. The only loose end is Professor Winston's role in all this. We aren't sure why he was at the scene where Miss Kramer supposedly retrieved information from Nick Boorstin."

"*What?*" Winston shouted. "You got it all wrong! The Russian was rendezvousing with Miss Kramer, and Miss Kramer and Thurston are involved in some sort of espionage!"

Chairman Yardley intervened. "So all we know for sure is that Professor Winston is being investigated, and Professor Thurston and Natalie Kramer have been cleared of any allegations of wrongdoing."

"Yes, sir," said agent Hargrove.

"Good work, Winston," declared McCracken, sarcastically.

"But that's ridiculous!" insisted Winston. "*I'm* the one who reported to the F.B.I. that something is going on."

"Give it up, Winston," said Yardley. "I'd like to nail Thurston for corruption or espionage or stealing supplies as much as the next person—"

"Amen!" interjected Anna Benson.

"—but you've got zilch. Any more business?"

"Yes," Thurston said. "As a professor in this department, this whole sordid mess that Professor Winston is involved in shocks me. I propose the department investigate Professor Winston to determine why he is spying on people, and making slanderous accusations against them."

"Don't push your luck," Yardley said. "Nothing else? ... Meeting adjourned."

Winston was still shell-shocked as he left the meeting.

"A masterful performance," McCracken told him. "I would say you successfully torpedoed any chance you had of being named department chairman."

"Don't worry about me, McCracken. I'll get this straightened out. My career isn't over. Washington still looks to me for advice."

"They won't when they find out the F.B.I. is investigating you for alleged ties to the Soviets," Thurston suggested. "They're sensitive about things like that. By the way, Winston. I read *Power Economics*. Were you high on cocaine when you wrote it?"

"I'd like to know the answer to that myself," said agent Hargrove.

34

July

BEFORE NATALIE AND Thurston embarked on the eight-city book tour Marcy Noble had set up for them, they showed up at the University Bookstore in Charlottesville for a special "book event". The Economics Department's four new authors were holding a joint book signing. Seated along a table surrounded by stacks of their books were Natalie Kramer, Gene Thurston, Glen McCracken and Herbert Winston.

When Thurston noticed the cover of McCracken's book, he was stunned.

"What language is that?" Thurston asked.

"Arabic."

الضرائب
القصة الكاملة

GLEN McCRACKEN

"What did they do, ship you the wrong copies of the book for the book signing?"

"Actually, there are no English copies. The only publisher I could find is located in Saudi Arabia. After this is over, I fly there for a book signing."

"I doubt if publishing your book in Arabic helped your chances of becoming the new department chairman. What does the cover say?"

"They tell me it says *Taxes: The Whole Story,* but it could say *American Professor Bares All* for all I know."

"Sometimes it's probably best we *don't* know what publishing houses do to our books," Thurston suggested.

"I couldn't agree more," said Natalie.

Thurston noticed no one was in line waiting for Winston to sign *Power Economics.* "Is the F.B.I. still shadowing you?" Thurston asked.

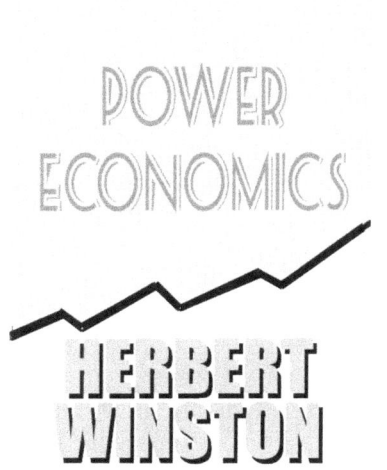

Winston cringed. "I did nothing wrong. I've put the whole mess behind me. There's just one thing I want to know ... which one of you sabotaged me at the Council of Economic Advisers meeting?"

McCracken smiled. "Herbert, life would be dull and monotonous if there were no mysteries. Some things are meant to remain mysteries forever."

"I hate you two," Winston muttered.

35

August

THE TIMING OF THE PUBLICATION of *End of the Road* could not have been better. In mid-August, right-wing hardliners ousted Mikhail Gorbachev as president of the Soviet Union, but the people would have none of it. They rallied around Russian Republic President Boris Yeltsin. With Yeltsin's backing, Gorbachev remained as president of the Soviet Union, but it was clear Yeltsin was calling the shots. The hardliners wanted to crush the rebellion, but Yeltsin called on the Russian people to resist. "You can build a throne out of bayonets, but you can't sit on them long," Yeltsin said.

In the end, the Russian people forced the defeat of the hardliners and the collapse of the Soviet Union.

End of the Road climbed to third place in the *New York Times* list of best-selling books. In a federal detention center in New York City, Nick noticed a story in *Newsday* reporting that Natalie Kramer and Eugene Thurston would be signing books at Oliver's Bookstore on Broadway that afternoon.

"I can make one phone call, right?" Nick asked his court-appointed attorney.

"Right."

Nick reached for a phone and called the bookstore. A young man named Anthony answered the phone.

"I need to talk to Natalie Kramer," Nick said.

"She's busy autographing copies of her book. Come in and buy a copy if you want to see her."

"That isn't possible," Nick grumbled, "for reasons a choir boy like you couldn't understand. ... She should *give me* damn book. *I* told her to write it. Let me talk to her!"

"Not possible. Sorry."

"Look, Anthony, I have friends who could torture and kill you and not lose any sleep over it. Let me talk to Kramer. *Now!*"

Nick's attorney was nervous, afraid someone had heard Nick. "Are you crazy? Aren't you facing enough charges?"

"One more won't make difference," Nick said.

Anthony told Natalie she had a phone call.

"Nick? I thought you were in prison."

"I am. You are making money off this book. I want my cut."

"Your cut? For what?"

"You wouldn't have written book if I didn't tell you to! Besides, if you don't pay me, I'll have Boris' cousin, Gregor, pay you visit. Next thing you know, you'll be screaming from pain in front of police station with vodka all over you and squad car will be going up in flames, and you will have lot of explaining to do. Would be easier to pay me, yes?"

"One thousand," Natalie said.

"*Ten* thousand," countered Nick. "And one-third of any movie deal you get."

"There won't be any movie deal. It's not that kind of book. Three thousand."

Nick hollered, *"Gregor! You busy? ... Got little job for you!"*

"Five thousand," said Natalie. "That's my *final* offer."

Nick sighed. "Okay. I take cashier's check. Don't take credit cards."

Nick told her where to mail the money.

"Moscow?" repeated Natalie. "You're going back to Moscow?"

"They're swapping all seven of us for seven Americans accused of spying. Don't know what they'll do to me in Moscow. They blame me for whole mess. The book. Crash of economy. Fall of Soviet Union. Everything. I am, what you call it, scapedog."

"Scapegoat," Natalie said.

"That too. But I will come out of this okay. Someday I will open automobile repair shop in Moscow.. Specialize in brake jobs."

36

September

The University of Virginia issued a press release announcing that Dean Freida Pensky had appointed a new chairman of the Department of Economics: Anna Benson.

A reporter interviewing Benson for the *Washington Post* asked what her first order of business would be.

"Investigating how I can kick Eugene Thurston out of the department. At the very least, I will make his life miserable. And I am ordering padlocks put on all the supply cabinets. Someone has been stealing us blind for years, and I think it's Thurston!"

The reporter called several professors in the department

to ask about their reactions to Anna Benson's appointment. Herbert Winston said, "It's a move up for Benson and let's hope she can handle it. I have already informed the dean that if anything happens to Benson—if she falls down a flight of stairs or is killed when someone crashes into her car—I would be available to serve as chairman."

Eugene Thurston's reaction was brief. "I think of myself as Sherlock Holmes and Benson as Professor Moriarty, the personification of all evil."

"Care to elaborate on that?"

"No."

October

Later that fall, Thurston married Natalie Kramer in a ceremony in Glen McCracken's spacious backyard. At the reception, he announced he was changing his area of specialization to Russian economics.

At about the same time, the F.B.I. reported it had closed its investigation into Herbert Winston's activities because of "insufficient evidence". Thurston tried to convince the F.B.I. to keep the investigation active, but the effort failed.

December

In December, the Soviet Union was declared dead and a commonwealth took its place.

Russia honored the seven spies who had been sent back to Russia by giving them medals. Nick Boorstin marked the occasion by offering a special on brake jobs at his new auto repair shop in Moscow.

NOTABLE NONFICTION
FINE FICTION
AND COOL HUMOR

WWW.MCNEILANDRICHARDS.COM

A THREE-WAY FIGHT FOR
A $2.5-MILLION-A-YEAR
ANCHOR JOB AS WAR RAGES
IN IRAQ IN 1991

WWW.MCNEILANDRICHARDS.COM

CAN THE LOSING CANDIDATE
BE STOPPED FROM STEALING
THE PRESIDENCY IN
IN THE ELECTORAL COLLEGE?

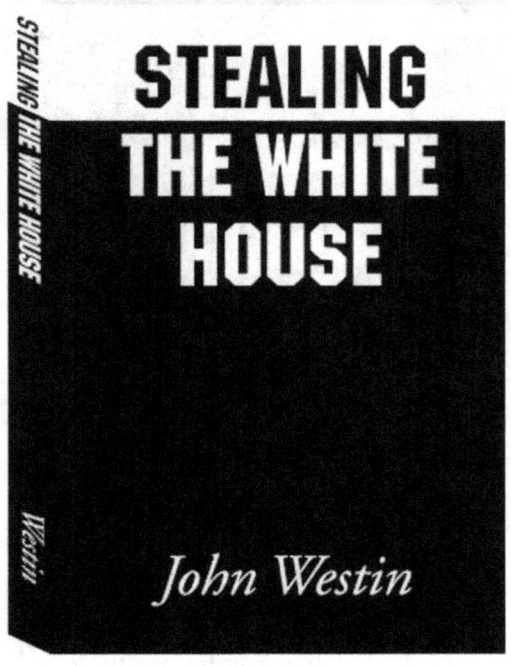

STEALING
THE WHITE
HOUSE

John Westin

STEALING THE WHITE HOUSE

Westin